ALEXANDRIA

OF

AFRICA

ALEXANDRIA
OF
AFRICA

ERIC WALTERS

DOUBLEDAY
CANADA

Doubleday Canada and colophon are trademarks.

Library and Archives Canada Cataloguing in Publication

Walters, Eric, 1957–
    Alexandria of Africa / Eric Walters.

ISBN 978-0-385-66639-8

    I. Title.
PS8595.A598A64 2008   jC813'.54   C2008-902250-5

Cover image: (zebra) Frank Krahmer / Taxi / Getty Images, (ostrich) © Steffen Foerster / Dreamstime.com
Cover design: Jennifer Lum
Printed and bound in Canada

Published in Canada by
Doubleday Canada, a division of
Random House of Canada Limited

Visit Random House of Canada Limited's website:
www.randomhouse.ca

TRANS   10   9   8   7   6   5   4   3   2   1

KENYA AND SURROUNDING COUNTRIES

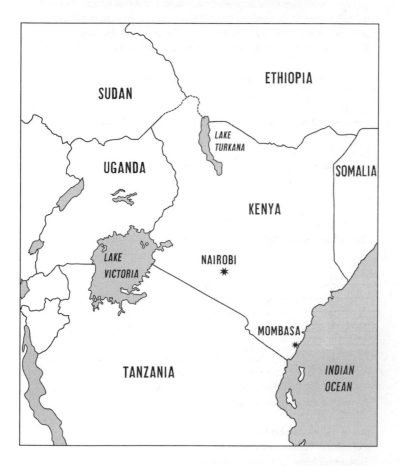

To the real Renée,

the real Nebala, Robin,

and all the incredible people at Free The Children,

who change lives

CHAPTER ONE

My mother tried to straighten the collar of my blouse and I brushed her hand away.

"I'm just trying to make sure you look all right," she said, sheepishly.

"I look as good as I can . . . in *this* outfit," I said. "But not as good as I could have looked if you hadn't picked out my clothes for me." I was just so glad that none of my friends were there to see me dressed like this: boring brown secretary skirt, white blouse with a Peter Pan collar, beige pantyhose, and flats . . . *shudder!*

My mother's style was pretty much classic—nothing but the best—but it was old-people fashion. She wasn't up on the latest.

"She was just doing what I instructed her to do," said my lawyer, Mr. Collins. "Appearance means a lot."

I huffed. I knew more about appearance than he *ever* would. The nerve of this man to decide how *I* should dress! Wrinkled suit, a stain on the tie, and the width of his lapels was so far out of fashion that it was almost back in again. For the amount of money my parents were paying him, you'd have thought he'd have the cash to dress better.

I heard the sound of a door opening and I spun around in time to see my father rushing in to the courtroom. Nice of him to find the time to make it.

"Sorry, traffic was terrible," he said.

Traffic is always terrible when you don't get into your car on time, I thought.

He came up and gave my mother a little kiss on the cheek. It looked really awkward. I hadn't seen them kiss for years *before* the divorce, so what was this all about? Were they putting on a show just for me, or demonstrating how sophisticated they were to people in general? *Divorced, but still friends.* It sounded like an episode for *Dr. Phil.*

Either way, it was just wrong on so many levels. Like a little show of affection was going to make me forget those last few years? The yelling and screaming, the threats, the household objects chucked at each other? I wasn't about to forget. In fact, I still used all that ammunition to my advantage. A little bit of guilt goes a long way, and a lot of guilt goes even further.

My mother didn't look well. She was really pale, and I thought she was even shaking a little. She looked so fragile. Whoever said it's impossible to be too thin never met my mother. She was painfully skinny. I always thought that a strong wind might blow her away and she'd just go flying off into the sky. Funny, she did look a bit like a bird.

My father glanced at his Rolex. "It looks like the judge got caught in traffic as well," he said. "Do you think he'll keep us waiting much longer?"

"His court, his time," Mr. Collins said.

"It had better not be long. I have places to get to," I said.

"You'd best put that attitude away, young lady," my father scolded.

I wanted to tell him that my attitude was something I'd inherited from him, but I didn't say a word. Never mind, I think my expression pretty well said it all.

"You just let your lawyer do the talking," my father warned me sternly.

"First I'm told how to dress, and now I'm not allowed to talk. Is it all right if I breathe the way I normally do?"

My father shot me a look, and I knew I'd be pushing it to say anything else, although I was severely tempted.

"She's just a little nervous, that's all," my mother said.

She put an arm around my shoulder but I edged away from her grasp.

"There's nothing to be afraid of," she continued.

"I'm not nervous, and I'm certainly not scared," I snapped.

"Maybe you *should* be afraid," my father said. "This isn't a joke. This is a court of law."

I started to chuckle but stopped myself. We both knew—we all knew—that my last trip to court was no big deal, just a slap on the wrist. It cost my parents time and a lot of money in legal fees, but for me it was nothing more than a minor inconvenience. This wouldn't be any different. It wasn't like I was going to get life in prison for stealing a couple of tops and a purse.

"I'm sure there's nothing to be concerned about," my mother said. She turned to my lawyer. "Right?"

"We can hope," he said.

"For the money I pay your firm I expect more than just *hope*," my father said. "I expect *certainty*."

"Nothing is certain in a court of law. The outcome is solely in the hands of the judge. You have to hope he's in a good mood . . . that he wasn't caught in traffic."

"I'm sure it will go just as well as the last time, sweetie," my mother said, soothingly.

"I'm afraid that might be the problem," said my lawyer. "Generally, judges are quite understanding the first time you appear before them, but I don't think Judge Roberts will be happy to see you in his court again so soon. Sometimes they feel that you're not just breaking the law but defying them. They take it very personally."

"How can he take it personally?" I asked. "It's not like I stole *his* clothes." *Unless he's wearing something frilly under that black robe,* I thought.

"But you did defy him by violating the terms of your probation," Mr. Collins said. "He might feel that, in essence, you lied to him."

"Lied? How did I lie?"

"You gave him your word that you would not break the law again. And yet here you are, less than two months later, back in his court."

"But it helps that she pleaded guilty in the pre-sentencing, right?" my mother asked.

"It certainly shows that she is willing to accept responsibility for her crime."

"Crime? I didn't kill anybody. I only took a few things, a few *little* things."

"Breaking the law and violating probation aren't generally considered 'little things' by most judges. They tend to take the law rather seriously. That's why they decided to become judges in the first place."

"And I even offered to pay for them right then and

there," I said. "I pulled the money out of my purse, but the store people wouldn't take it."

"Stores usually operate on the premise that you pay willingly for their products, not simply offer to pay if you get caught trying to take them. They're funny that way."

Now I was getting attitude from my lawyer! Actually, where was my *real* lawyer? Why did I have this junior associate instead of the lawyer I'd had the first time I was in court? This guy was way too young to be a lawyer. And how good could he be if he couldn't afford better clothes, or shoes that didn't look like they came from Payless?

"You need to know that this could be serious," he said.

"Whatever," I snapped. "What's he going to do, throw me in prison?"

There was an uneasy silence and I felt a shiver go up my spine. I looked from my mother to my father. Both were looking at the floor and not at me.

"He can't send me to prison . . . can he?" I asked my lawyer.

He smiled. "Of course not."

I felt a rush of relief. How stupid of me to even think—

"Prison is only for adult offenders. You'd be sent to juvenile detention."

The anxiety came rushing back, only worse.

"Could you please explain to us what juvenile detention is?" my father asked.

"It's a secure setting for young people who have committed crimes but are not old enough to be placed in an adult facility, i.e., a jail."

"What does that mean, *secure* setting?" I asked.

"Locked doors, bars on the windows, locked rooms."

"But that sounds like a jail!"

"It is," he said. "It's a kiddie jail. Cells, guards, no personal possessions, including, of course, no telephones." He pointed at my purse. He'd made me turn off my phone and stash it in my purse because it had been ringing so much while we were waiting to come into court. Was it my fault that I was popular?

"You would share a room with two or three other prisoners," he continued.

"I'd be with prisoners?" I gasped.

"You would *be* a prisoner."

"Mr. Collins, isn't that a little bit harsh?" my mother asked.

He shook his head. "That's what they're called. People who are in detention are prisoners. Most rooms have one or two sets of bunk beds and a shared toilet in the corner."

"The toilet is in the *room?* That's . . . that's just *disgusting!*"

"And, of course, you're issued a standard detention uniform."

"You mean I couldn't wear my own clothing?" I gasped. "But what would I wear?"

"Everybody dresses in the same jumpsuit."

"But nobody wears jumpsuits any more! They're so yesterday!"

"That's what they wear. Orange jumpsuits."

"Oh God! I look awful in orange! *Everybody* looks awful in orange!" I felt my lower lip start to quiver. I was on the verge of tears—the real kind, not the trying to-get-my-own-way type!

"Please, Mr. Collins, there's no point in getting into any of this," my mother said. She wrapped an arm around me. This time I didn't brush it away.

"It's my job to let you know what might happen," he said.

"But you're scaring her!"

"Still, detention time is one of the possibilities."

"How possible?" my father asked.

"It's hard to say."

"Ballpark it for me. What do you think the odds are of her serving time?"

"Umm . . . I hate to make a prediction . . . maybe less than a 10 percent chance."

"I like those odds," my father said. "I'll always take a business deal where there's a 90 percent chance of success."

Suddenly this had become a business deal? I didn't know whether I should be honoured or insulted. After all, I knew how much his business meant to him.

"And if it all did go south and she was sent to detention, what sort of time would we be talking about?" he asked.

"There are established guidelines for each offence, but the judge has a lot of discretion within those guidelines."

"So, what's the worst-case scenario? How bad could the damage be?"

"Up to six months."

"Six months!" I exclaimed as I jumped to my feet. "That's crazy! It was just a few things! It wasn't like I killed somebody! I'll tell the judge I won't do it again!"

"Unfortunately, that's what you told him the last time," Mr. Collins said.

"Anyway, just calm down," my father said. "You can't lose your cool. People smell fear in business deals."

"This is my *life,* not a *business deal!*" I protested.

"*Everything* is a business deal. Besides, we're not talking about what *will* happen, just what *could* happen."

"But you won't let me go to juvenile detention, will you, Daddy?" I pleaded.

"Your father has very little say in this," Mr. Collins said before my father could answer.

"But still, six months for shoplifting, that makes no sense," my mother argued.

"This wouldn't just be for shoplifting. It would include the charge of violating probation and also the reinstatement of the original charge of vandalism."

"How can that be fair?" I protested. "I even paid for her car to be repaired."

"Your father paid," Mr. Collins said. "And that doesn't change the fact that you pummelled a car with a golf club, causing thousands of dollars in damage and terrifying the girl who was in the car during your temper tantrum."

Hey, it wasn't a temper tantrum. It was about getting even, getting back, not letting somebody get away with something. I almost smiled at the memory. She deserved to have a golf club taken to her car. Now that little tramp would think twice before trying to steal anybody's boyfriend again.

"A lot will depend on the pre-sentence report, prepared by the court-appointed social worker," Mr. Collins explained.

"Have you seen it?" my father asked him.

"It's only for the judge to see." Mr. Collins turned to me. "Do you have a sense of what the report might say?"

"How would I know?"

"The social worker did interview you. You were there."

"Of course I was there," I snapped.

"Well, how did the interview go?"

"It went fine . . . I guess."

"You guess?" my father asked.

"Well, she was late and I had an appointment to have

my hair done and I couldn't hang around." I turned to my mom. "You know how hard it is to get an appointment with Mr. Henri and how angry he gets when you're even a minute late."

"He can throw quite the little hissy fit," my mother confirmed.

"Please don't tell me you blew off the interview because of some haircut!" Mr. Collins exclaimed.

"First off, it was a *style,* not a *cut.*" I almost said something about him *desperately* needing a good stylist because apparently he cut his own hair, but that was beside the point. "And second, I *did* do the interview."

My lawyer let out a big sigh of relief.

"Although I refused to answer some of her questions."

The shocked look on my lawyer's face actually startled me.

"Well, some of her questions were just so *personal.* I thought, Who does she think she is? What right did she have to ask *me* questions?"

"She had the right to ask you anything she wanted," Mr. Collins said. "She had the authority of the court! She was asking the questions that the judge wanted the answers to!"

"It wasn't just the questions," I said. "It was the way she asked them. She was totally rude. She had quite the attitude."

"*She* had an attitude?" Mr. Collins questioned.

I knew what he was implying but I chose to show some class and ignore him.

"Yes, the nerve of some woman who shops at Wal-Mart, and doesn't even have the sense to have her bag match her shoes, to think that she could sit there and judge me!"

Mr. Collins put his head down on the table. How unprofessional! Not to mention that from that angle his hair was even less flattering. Forget the hairstyle, a shampoo would have been helpful for a start.

The door off to the side of the bench sprang open and a large man in a uniform came in.

"All rise for the Honourable Judge Roberts!"

CHAPTER TWO

We all stood up as the judge entered the room. He was followed by another man in uniform, a man in a suit, and a woman with absolutely no sense of fashion. She was wearing the clunkiest shoes I'd ever seen, and her skirt and blouse didn't go together at all. If the fashion police had been able to make arrests she'd have been in court for an entirely different reason. She went over to a table in the corner. She was the court secretary, so she was there to take notes and stuff.

The judge took his seat behind the high wooden bench.

"Please be seated," Judge Roberts said.

My lawyer and I took our places at the table and my parents sat down directly behind us. The man with the suit took the table beside ours. The two guys in uniform stood on either side of the judge, like they were guarding him. Did anybody really think I was going to assault the judge?

"Court is now in session," the court secretary said. "Our first matter involves a charge of theft under $500, shoplifting, and a violation of probation. The defendant is Alexandria Hyatt."

"That name sounds familiar," the judge said, his eyes still focused on the papers on the bench in front of him.

People usually remembered me.

" . . . and that is not a good thing," he added, looking up and staring directly at me.

My lawyer got to his feet. "Mr. Collins, representing Ms. Hyatt."

"If I'm not mistaken, you were not the lawyer of record on Ms. Hyatt's previous charge."

"No, sir, that would have been Mr. Kruger, the senior partner in my firm."

"Yes," Judge Roberts said. "I recall how peculiar it was to have a senior partner of a major firm representing a juvenile on a first offence."

"The defendant's father and his business holdings are major clients of the firm, and he requested that Mr. Kruger be present at that hearing," Mr. Collins explained.

"Must be nice to have pull," Judge Roberts said, looking at my father.

I knew that would make him happy.

"Although obviously not enough pull to have Mr. Kruger make the return appearance," the judge went on.

That my father wouldn't like. I would have liked to turn around to see his expression. Hardly anybody ever spoke to him like that . . . really, nobody but my mother, and that was only before the divorce.

"Mr. Kruger was unfortunately unable to attend as he is presently in Hong Kong negotiating some sensitive arrangements on behalf of Ms. Hyatt's father."

"So, Mr. Hyatt wanted to make sure his business dealings were taken care of, rather than . . ."

He let the sentence trail off but I knew what he meant—instead of me. I hadn't thought of that.

"Could I ask, Mr. Collins, how long you have been a partner in the firm?"

Mr. Collins laughed. "I'm not a partner, Your Honour. I'm one of the firm's most junior lawyers."

"Shocking!" Judge Roberts said, although his tone and expression were far from shocked. He actually sounded kind of amused. Maybe that could work in my favour—a judge in a good mood could only mean good things.

"And did the rest of the senior partners and all the junior partners and associates also accompany Mr. Kruger on his trip?"

"Um . . . no, sir."

"Did you wonder how the *honour* of representing Ms. Hyatt fell to you?" the judge asked.

"No, sir. I was asked by one of my superiors."

"Which must be almost everybody in the firm, with the possible exception of the mailroom staff and the guy who makes coffee. Mr. Collins, are you familiar with the term 'sacrificial goat,' or perhaps the admonition, 'Don't shoot the messenger'?"

"Um, both, Your Honour. The latter arises from a fear that the person who delivers bad news might somehow be held responsible for the content of the message and punished accordingly. He, in essence, becomes the sacrificial goat. But I don't see how this applies to my being—"

"You might see the connection soon enough. Sit down."

Mr. Collins took the seat beside me. I had no idea what any of this meant but I got the feeling that Judge Roberts wasn't any more impressed with Mr. Collins than I was.

The judge was acting a little strangely, though. He certainly wasn't the way I remembered him from the first time I was in court. And there was a peculiar look in his eyes. They looked almost . . . glazed.

"Perhaps before I continue I should apologize for my tardiness. I personally detest being kept waiting and consider it the height of unprofessional behaviour to keep others waiting."

"That's okay," I said, and smiled at the judge.

"That is so gracious of you, Ms. Hyatt. I was particularly worried about keeping *you* waiting."

"Me?"

"Yes, I was afraid you might have to leave . . . as you did, apparently, when the pre-sentence report was being prepared."

I swallowed hard. This was not a good sign.

"As well, I recall at your last appearance that you looked somewhat distracted, dare I say even . . . bored?"

"Not bored," I said. "Although I guess things could have moved a tad more quickly."

"Again, my apologies. I'll try my best to keep things moving, and I'll certainly make sure you aren't bored this time."

There was a tone in his voice and glint in his eyes that sort of scared me.

"I just wanted to make sure I wasn't keeping you from something more important, something like a hair appointment."

That woman had obviously said something about that in her report.

"By the way, your hair does look *fantastic!* My compliments to your stylist."

"Thank you." I'd worked on it for over an hour that morning. If I couldn't wear the clothes I wanted, at least my hair could be right, and it was nice of him to notice.

"Mr. Collins, perhaps you could have Ms. Hyatt pass on to you the name of her stylist."

"I'm afraid he really doesn't take new referrals," I said. "He's pretty exclusive."

"What a pity. Poor Mr. Collins is destined to spend his life appearing as though he is far more concerned with what is *in* his head than what is on *top* of it. I imagine that isn't a concern you have been accused of having, Ms. Hyatt."

"No," I said. I wasn't exactly sure what he meant, but I had to agree with his assessment of my lawyer's haircut.

"But I digress. The reason I was late was because I had to see my doctor. You might have noticed this." He pulled his robe down slightly to reveal a thick white collar around his neck. I had noticed the white, but I'd assumed he was wearing a scarf. This was no scarf. It was the sort of thing people wore when they had a neck injury . . . it was called whip . . . ship . . . something.

"I am suffering from a case of whiplash," he said.

"That's it!" I exclaimed, without thinking.

"My doctor will be so glad that you agree with his diagnosis. Have you ever had whiplash, Ms. Hyatt?"

I shook my head and then stopped. Maybe that was like showing off that I *could* move my head.

"Any of you?" he asked.

There was a general shaking of heads.

"You are all very fortunate. It's not pleasant. In fact, it's rather painful. If I didn't have medication I'd be in constant pain." He held up a little bottle of pills and shook it. "Now I'm going to share with you all how I received this injury. Very informative." He paused and looked directly at me. "Ms. Hyatt, this story isn't boring you, is it?"

"No." It *was* starting to get a little long, but I wasn't going to say anything. I wasn't stupid or rude.

"Good. I was driving along when I made the terrible mistake of stopping at a red light. How, you might be asking yourselves, could this be a mistake? It was a mistake because the car behind me decided that the red light was merely a suggestion and plowed into the rear of my car."

"How awful," I said.

"How kind of you to feel that way. Actually, in all fairness, it wasn't that the driver made a conscious decision to go through that light. She surely knew that red means stop and green means go, but she failed to see either the light or my car stopped at it. She was, in fact, doing what my kids like to call 'multi-tasking.' Mr. Hyatt, a successful businessman such as yourself must be very adept at this practice."

"It's part of the job description of any successful CEO."

"Then apparently I must have been rear-ended by a future Fortune 500 CEO, because this young lady was not only driving, she was also talking on her cellphone and, this is truly remarkable, retouching her nails!"

Not that impressive. Everybody I knew stripped them down and reapplied. Retouching nails was so tacky!

"And all of this at the tender age of sixteen while driving her father's very expensive car. Do you drive your father's car, Ms. Hyatt?"

"My client is only fifteen," Mr. Collins said.

"I know her age, Mr. Collins. It's all in this report," he said, holding up some papers. "My question is, have you ever driven your father's car?"

"Well . . ."

"I let her drive in parking lots," my father said, jumping to his feet. "I'm just helping her to become a better driver, the sort that wouldn't crash into a judge's car. She'll be sixteen soon."

"And then she'll drive your car," the judge said. He paused. "Or will you be buying her a car of her own?"

"Well, I was thinking that might be a possibility."

I knew it was more than a possibility. It was a locked-down, guaranteed thing. I expected a car to be waiting at the end of the driveway on the morning of my birthday. I'd been taking driver's education and had already spent time behind the wheel of a car. I was a pretty good driver already.

"So, back to my story. This young lady rammed my car, and do you know what she was most concerned about? The air bag, which probably saved her from injury, had smashed her sunglasses . . . her *Versace* sunglasses."

I could understand how that would hurt.

"Do you have Versace sunglasses, Ms. Hyatt?"

I shook my head. I didn't like the look. I had a pair of Guccis and a really cute little pair from Chanel. I looked *so* good in those.

"Perhaps your mother could buy you a pair to go along with your new car. But again, I digress. My point is, this young lady didn't care if I was injured. She didn't care that two cars were badly damaged or that countless lives might have been put at risk. Aside from her distress over the sunglasses, she showed no remorse or concern. None!"

He practically yelled out those last few words, which startled me a bit.

"And do you know why I decided to tell you this story?"

Again I shook my head. I had no idea, although I had to admit he hadn't been boring.

"Because of this report," he said, as he slammed it down on the bench in front of him. "You, Ms. Hyatt, are without remorse!"

Mr. Collins jumped to his feet. "Your Honour, my client is willing to plead guilty and she has offered to pay for the merchandise and she feels terrible about what has—"

"Sit down, Mr. Collins! You know full well that your client feels terrible only about getting caught. You're here to speak on her behalf, not to issue bald-faced lies believed by no one."

Meekly, Mr. Collins sat down beside me.

"My report also states that you have been expelled from three private schools."

"But she's doing very well in her new school," my mother chimed in.

"Is she? And how long has she been in attendance at this latest school?"

"It's been almost two months," my mother answered sheepishly.

"That is quite the accomplishment. Let's organize a parade and declare a national holiday!"

"There's no need for that tone or attitude!" my father said.

The judge slammed his hand against the bench. I jumped, and my mother let out a little shriek.

"Mr. Collins, please advise your client's family member to keep his comments to himself. Otherwise he will either be escorted from the court or he will find himself in contempt."

"Well, if that isn't—"

"I will apologize for Mr. Hyatt," Mr. Collins said, turning around to face my father and gesturing for him to be calm and silent.

"Now, back to the reason for our little gathering. Ms. Hyatt, you readily admit to stealing the items. There is no argument, correct?"

"Yeah."

"I appreciate that. You are a thief but not a liar. Good

for you. And my report states that when you were appre-hended you had over four hundred dollars in your purse. You must have a very lucrative job."

I shook my head. "I don't have a job. I'm only fifteen."

"Then how did you come to have such a large sum of money? Are you a drug dealer?"

"Your Honour, I ob—"

"Mr. Collins, I wasn't seriously thinking that your client was a drug dealer. Dealing drugs would involve actual work. I was just curious as to how she got such a sum."

"It's my allowance."

"You get a four-hundred-dollar allowance?"

"No, that was two weeks' allowance," I said.

"Only two hundred dollars a week—however do you get by on that?"

I could tell that he was mocking me. He was just upset because he couldn't be that generous with his children. After all, how much could a judge make? Certainly not the sort of money my father did.

"So the question I really want answered is very simple. If you had that amount of money, and you knew that each week you would receive your allowance, why did you not simply pay for the items you stole?"

I shrugged.

"Not the most articulate answer. Think again, because this, Ms. Hyatt, is perhaps the most important answer you have given thus far in your young life. Why did you choose to steal these items?"

"Well . . ."

"Well, what?"

"Well, I guess I just wanted them."

"But why did you not simply pay for them? You had the money."

"I guess I didn't want to."

"And," he said, "I imagine that you are accustomed to always getting what you want, correct?"

"I guess, a lot of the time."

"Then today is going to be quite a shock for you, Ms. Hyatt. To quote that eminent philosopher and rock and roll legend Mr. Mick Jagger, you can't always get what you want, but sometimes you get what you need."

I gave him a confused look. What sort of judge quoted rock musicians? I looked directly at him. Was he leaning slightly to one side? And there was something about his eyes—he looked a little wild.

"If we consider your previous offence, the violation of probation, the new charges, and the fact of your having been expelled from a number of schools, a consistent pattern emerges. In my court, money does not buy justice or influence. Do you understand where this is going, Ms. Hyatt? Do you have even a hint of the fall that is about to happen? Are you aware that you are about to face the consequences of your actions?"

"Whatever," I muttered.

"What a surprise that you gave that response. It's the same answer you gave to twelve separate questions in this report. It is the answer given by somebody who either doesn't care or is simply not bright enough to understand the situation. Are you stupid, Ms. Hyatt?"

"You can't speak to my daughter like that!" my father thundered.

"I can speak to anybody in my court in any way I wish. Bailiff, if that man opens his mouth again, even to breathe, I order you to remove him from the court and place him in a holding cell!"

My father's mouth snapped shut. He looked

unnerved—no, he actually looked frightened. I'd never seen my father with that expression before. This man was starting to scare me.

"It is about time somebody spoke to you this way," the judge said. "It is time that somebody spoke to this whole dysfunctional family this way. Unfortunately, only one of you is technically before the court today, and I'm going to do that person an incredible favour."

Favour . . . he was going to do me a favour?

"Ms. Hyatt, stand up."

I got to my feet.

"Ms. Hyatt, for this charge, the breach of probation, and the original charge being reinstated, I am sentencing you to juvenile detention for a period of one hundred and twenty days."

"What?" I gasped, not able to believe my ears. "But . . . but you said you were doing me a favour."

"Believe me, I am. This is exactly what you need."

"No," I said, shaking my head. "I don't need that and I'm not going. I'm going home, right now!"

I started to get up, but Mr. Collins grabbed me by the arm and pulled me back down. Whose side was he on, anyway?

"Let go of me!" I screamed. "You can't touch me!"

He released his grip.

"And you can't tell me what to do!" I yelled at the judge. "You're not my parent!"

He laughed. "Apparently, nobody has ever been a parent to you. Well, for perhaps the first time in your precious little life you're finally going to get what you need rather than what you want. Bailiff, remove Ms. Hyatt and place her in a holding cell."

CHAPTER THREE

I sat on the bed—if you could call the thin, lumpy piece of material lying on the metal platform a bed. With my arms wrapped around my knees, holding them tightly to my chest, I was rocking back and forth. I'd tried to stop myself a few times but I just kept doing it. At least I'd finally stopped crying. My eyes were all puffy, and my nose was stuffed up—thank goodness! I couldn't imagine how much worse that toilet would have smelled otherwise. It stood there in the corner of the room, staring at me. I didn't care how badly I had to go, I would never use that thing! I'd just wait until I got home and . . . *home* . . . I felt the tears starting to come again.

"Ms. Hyatt?"

I looked up. There on the other side of the bars was Mr. Collins. I was so relieved to see him I wanted to jump up and rush over and . . . there beside him was that nasty gorilla of a bailiff. On his cheek was a bandage covering the place where I'd raked my nails across his face. He'd won, but I'd put up a fight, and he had the marks to show for it! The only regret I had was that one of my expensive silk gel nails had come off in the scuffle. That was just another thing to add to the bill when we sued these people!

"Are you all right?" Mr. Collins asked.

"Do I look all right?" I demanded. I bit down hard on the inside of my cheek to hold back the tears.

Slowly I stood up, holding on to the bed with one hand to steady myself. The coarse material of the pants they'd given me scratched against my shaking legs.

"Those female guards took my clothes," I whimpered.

"No choice," the bailiff said. "There was a belt in your skirt."

"What has that got to do with anything?" I demanded. "That outfit needed a belt as a contrast to the—"

"They didn't want you to have anything that you could use to hang yourself," Mr. Collins explained.

"Hang myself? Why would they think I would do that?" Obviously somebody thought I might. "Well, how about my makeup? They took that away, too. Did they think I was going to stab myself with my eyeliner?"

"No personal items allowed," the bailiff said.

"I must look a mess," I moaned.

Neither of them answered, which was, I guess, an answer. I knew my makeup would have run down my cheeks with the tears. I hated looking that way, but almost as much I hated wearing the evidence that they'd made me cry. How awful did I look? The cell didn't even have a mirror. Now *that* was cruel and unusual punishment.

"We can't do anything about how you look," Mr. Collins said, "but we might be able to do something about the larger issue. Come on."

The bailiff pulled out his keys and opened the cell.

"I'm going home?" I asked, not daring to believe it.

"You're going to go to a meeting to discuss if going home is an option," Mr. Collins explained.

"Is *he* going to be there?" I said, pointing to the bailiff.

"He will be escorting you to the meeting and supervising you."

"If *he's* going, then *I'm* not."

"Works for me," the bailiff said. He slammed the door shut with a loud clang.

"Wait!" I screamed. "If I don't go to this meeting, what happens to me?"

"Simple. You stay here until they make arrangements for you to be transported to the detention centre, where you will start to serve your sentence," Mr. Collins explained.

"And if I come to this meeting?"

"You could possibly go home."

"I could . . . really?"

"Of course, that also depends on whether or not additional charges are filed against you."

"How can they charge me with anything else? I've been locked inside this cell!"

"Resisting arrest and assaulting a court officer, to begin with," Mr. Collins said.

"But he started it!"

"The bailiff was following a court order. He was allowed to remove you to the holding cell. That's partly why it's important for him to be part of this meeting. The decision to press the assault charge or not is his and his alone."

I was dead.

"And he's agreed to consider not pressing charges."

"Really?"

"Really," the bailiff said.

"Which is pretty generous," Mr. Collins added. "I know if it were me and my face I'd want them to throw the book at you."

"You're not supposed to say things like that! You're my lawyer!" I protested.

"I'm here to represent your best interests, and I'm beginning to agree with the judge that your interests might ultimately be best served by a stint in detention."

"You think I should go to detention?" I gasped.

"The jury is still out on that one. Regardless, are you going to come to this meeting or not?"

"I'm thinking about it."

"Think all you want. But what you should be thinking about is that the rest of us are all going home tonight," he said.

I felt as if somebody had thrown a glass of cold water in my face. "Okay, I'm coming."

The bailiff opened the door again. I stepped out and took a deep breath. Somehow the air on this side of the bars seemed better.

Mr. Collins led, I followed, and the bailiff walked behind me. We passed down a long corridor lined on both sides with cells. There were loud conversations, people laughing, crying, swearing, and yelling. I dared to glance at one cell as we passed. It was filled with people. I couldn't imagine there were that many female criminals in the entire world. At least they'd given me a private cell.

We entered an elevator and the doors closed on the noise. The ride ended and we exited into a quiet carpeted, wood-panelled corridor. It was as though we'd taken an elevator ride from hell to a hotel. A very nice hotel.

Mr. Collins opened a door and gestured for me to enter. I stepped through and—

"Alexandria!" my mother screamed. She rushed over and threw her arms around me. I buried my face into her shoulder. My father wrapped his arms around both of us.

"Could everybody please take a seat," Mr. Collins said.

I released my grip and my father guided me into one of the chairs lined up around a big wooden conference table. He and my mother took seats on either side of me. Mr. Collins and that other man in a suit from the courtroom took seats on the other side.

"Let's get down to business," Mr. Collins said. "Some of us need to be getting home." He gave me a look as though he was quite amused with his little joke. "Ms. Hyatt, this gentleman is Mr. Livingston, and he is the district attorney in this case. The judge has given him the power to negotiate on his behalf."

"Judge Roberts has gone home," Mr. Livingston said. "He wasn't feeling well."

"I want this whole thing investigated!" my father thundered. "That man, that judge had no right to say the things he said or—"

"You'll be saying nothing bad against the judge!" the bailiff yelled. "He's one of the finest men I've ever had the honour to serve under!"

Mr. Livingston raised his hands. "It's all right, Harry." He turned back to us. "Judge Roberts is one of the finest jurists I have ever been involved with. I think we can all agree that perhaps the medication he is taking to control the pain may have affected his behaviour somewhat today."

"And on those grounds, do we not have the right to appeal his sentence?" my father asked.

"You do."

"Mr. Collins, I want you to launch an appeal immediately, and I want Mr. Kruger to put the entire weight of the firm behind that appeal!"

My father would show them they couldn't push either of us around.

"You might want to reconsider an appeal," Mr. Collins said.

"Why in heaven's name wouldn't we appeal? Are you suggesting that we simply allow our little girl to remain in jail?"

"Appealing the case might result in your daughter spending a much longer period of time in detention," Mr. Collins said.

"I don't understand," my father said.

"Let me explain," Mr. Livingston said. "You can appeal the sentence. That appeal could take a month—"

"Or longer," Mr. Collins said.

"Or longer," he agreed. "And pending that appeal, your daughter will remain in detention."

"That's outrageous!" my father said.

"But legally correct," Mr. Livingston replied.

"There must be something that can be done," my father said to Mr. Collins.

"Nothing," Mr. Livingston replied. "Your daughter will be held in custody pending the other charges she is now potentially facing. Those charges include resisting arrest and assault on a court officer."

"The courts really, really don't like it when you assault their own," Mr. Collins said. "She'll be in jail until the appeal happens."

"And it is pretty well guaranteed that she will be convicted of both of those new charges. Add those to her existing criminal record, and I would say that a period of detention of around one year could be expected."

My whole stomach did a flip and I felt as though I was going to be sick.

"But there is another alternative," Mr. Livingston said.

"I'm listening," my father said.

We were all listening. Maybe harder than I'd ever listened to anything in my whole life.

"You agree not to launch an appeal or question, in any way, today's proceedings. In exchange, no further criminal charges will be laid against your daughter and she will not be sentenced to detention as a result of the charges that brought her before the courts today. You can take your daughter home."

"I can go home?"

"You can go home, but there is a catch. You must agree to be part of a diversion program."

"What does that mean?" I asked.

"Diversion programs are designed for people who are not habitual criminals. The idea is to divert them away from criminal behaviours and to keep them out of the criminal justice system. They offer a constructive alternative to detention."

"So, I wouldn't have to go back into a place like that cell, right?"

"No cell, no detention centre, no new charges filed, and in fact your criminal record for the shoplifting would be erased."

"And what would my daughter be doing instead?" my father asked.

I didn't care what I was going to be doing. Anything had to be better.

"She would be placed under the care of an organization

called Child Save. It's a charity that works to improve the lives of children. What she would be doing would depend on the mission she was assigned to."

"I know this organization, and I've spoken to people who have gone on their trips," Mr. Collins said.

"Trips?" I asked.

"Yes, this is an international organization that does work in countries around the world. Is that a problem?" Mr. Collins asked.

"No, I love to travel!"

"It's a problem for me!" my mother protested. "You can't expect me to simply allow my baby to be sent to some place on the other side of the planet without her mother!" She grabbed my hand.

"Your 'baby' is almost sixteen, Mrs. Hyatt, and perhaps it's time she had an opportunity to stand on her own two feet," Mr. Livingston said. "But if you insist, she can certainly stay right here, close to home, in a safe, secure detention centre."

I pulled my hand away from my mother's. "I'm not afraid of travelling."

"I think it would be a good opportunity for your daughter," Mr. Collins said. "And, quite frankly, I see that she is in desperate need of something."

"What are you implying?" my father asked.

"This is not an implication as much as a fact. Your daughter is a spoiled, egocentric brat."

"How dare you say that about Alexandria!" my mother objected.

"You're on pretty thin ice," my father threatened. "Do you like your job, Mr. Collins?"

"Today, not particularly," he said, shaking his head.

"Do you think Mr. Kruger will be pleased with you

when he hears you've insulted the daughter of one of his biggest clients?"

"Probably not, but I assume he'd be even more upset to discover that you have threatened the son of his only sister. Mr. Kruger is my uncle."

"Your uncle?"

"My Uncle Stan. And one of the things my uncle admires most about me is my honesty. And that's what I'm giving you. Honesty. This isn't just about the easy way out, Mr. Hyatt. It's about the right way out."

"There are also a few other considerations," Mr. Livingston said. "The diversion program is expensive. You would be responsible for airfare and the cost of lodging."

"Cost is no object when it comes to my daughter," my father said.

"Second, she might have to leave on very short notice, perhaps only a few days."

"Again, not an issue."

"Third, your daughter will be expected to follow the direction of the Child Save staff. If she fails to do so, she will be forfeiting the agreement."

"What does that mean?" I asked.

"You will end up right back here in court, and then you *will* go to detention," Mr. Collins said. "Except this time you will have no way out. You will go to detention and you can expect to spend a year there."

"And I will do my utmost to make sure the sentence is at least that long," Mr. Livingston said.

"You can't threaten us," my father said.

"That wasn't a threat. I believe people need to be given fair warning of the consequences of their actions. That will be the consequence of your daughter failing to hold up her end of the deal."

"It still sounds like a threat," my father muttered.

"Think of it as more of a promise. And you have," Mr. Livingston said, looking at his watch, "one minute to make your decision."

"One minute! That's ridiculous!"

"Perhaps you're right," he said, and he broke into a smile. "It's Friday, almost four-thirty. Why don't you take the weekend to think it over?"

"That certainly sounds more reasonable."

"I'm glad you think so. And while you're home thinking this through, your daughter will be transferred to the detention facility. Bailiff, please remove her again to the holding cell."

"We'll take it!" I yelled. "I'll go to that program!"

Mr. Livingston nodded his head. "Do we all agree?"

"I believe that we are being blackmailed," my father said.

"Blackmail is a criminal offence. We are simply negotiating . . . playing hardball . . . I'm sure you've done that a few times in your business dealings. So, Mr. Hyatt, do we have a deal or don't we?"

My father didn't answer. I couldn't tell if he was thinking or had already made up his mind to put up a fight, because he hated to be pressured and he hated to lose. But the only person here who was really going to lose was me. He had to say yes, he had to agree. Slowly he nodded his head.

"We have a deal."

CHAPTER FOUR

My phone burst into song once more. It had hardly stopped all day. The price of being popular. Sprout, my little Pomeranian pup, was perched on my lap. I scooped her up in my arms and walked over to pick up the phone from the dresser.

"Talk to me," I said as I answered it.

"Alexandria, is it true?"

It was Olivia. She was somebody I *knew*, as opposed to somebody I really *liked*. She was just so pretentious. She thought she was just *so* special. She was seriously annoying.

"Tell me what you've heard and I'll tell you if it's true."

"Don't be so coy. Africa, you're going to Africa."

"I am. For three weeks."

"Unbelievable. Only you could be charged with something and end up getting a vacation out of it. You are untouchable."

I didn't answer. Instead I checked out the small

bruise on my arm where the doctor had given me the immunizations. Yellow fever, typhoid, meningitis, hepatitis, and rabies. "Untouchable" wasn't quite the word I'd have used.

"I was so upset when you got arrested . . . again."

I'd heard she was delighted and told people I was finally going to get what I deserved. She was so two-faced. What *she* deserved was to have a golf club taken to her new little car.

"Wouldn't want to make a habit of getting arrested," she teased.

Better than her habit of being dropped by boyfriend after boyfriend. The only way she could hold on to a boyfriend was by tying one up and locking him in her closet.

"So, when do you leave?"

"Tomorrow. Well, at least I'm flying to Paris tomorrow."

"Paris," she gasped.

"Yes, a very exciting city. Have you ever been?"

"No," she said.

I already knew that she'd never been to Paris. I just wanted to make a point.

"This will be my third time. You should go some day . . . you know . . . in the future." I paused for dramatic effect. I plopped down on the edge of my bed and Sprout snuggled into my arm.

"I imagine you'll do some shopping," Olivia said.

"I'll do a little, but not much. My mother already took me out yesterday and practically wore out her credit cards. She bought me almost everything new that I might need." Guilt was a powerful tool, and my mother was really feeling guilty about the whole thing.

"That sounds amazing," Olivia said, but her voice lacked enthusiasm. I guess what she was saying was that it would have been amazing if it had been her. I knew she had to be almost green already, but I had more.

"Could you be a darling and make sure you keep the evening of the twenty-fourth open? My parents are throwing me a little thing to celebrate my return *and* my birthday. Nothing too big, just a hundred or so people. I wanted it smaller but I just couldn't without offending somebody. You know how it is to be popular."

At least more popular than she was. Her sixteenth had been two months ago and she'd only had fifty people show up.

"I'll have to get back to you on that. It's awfully short notice and I'll have to check my schedule," she said. "But really, darling, I'll try to at least drop in, you know, make an appearance."

That little snob was trying to make it look as if she was doing me a favour by coming to my party! I'd show her.

"I saw you with your new car," I said. She'd gotten it from her parents as her Sweet Sixteen present. "It's such a cute little thing . . . a Mustang, right?"

"Yes, it is."

"I don't know much about cars, it's just that our maid drives the *exact* same one." I had to fight not to laugh. "Even the same colour. Matter of fact, the first time you drove by I waved because I thought it was Carmella, and then it turned out to be you. What a surprise!"

"Enjoy your trip," she said coldly. "I have to go."

"I will. And you enjoy your car. Later."

I hung up. I'd teach her to mess with me. There was only room for one princess, and that wasn't her. Her and her cheesy little Mustang—who drove anything that was American-made? I was certain that my father was going to get me something better than that. Well, almost certain.

Maybe, I thought, I shouldn't let chance play a role. I'd just tell him that Fred Mason got his daughter Olivia a Mustang for her birthday. He didn't like the father any more than I liked the daughter. I could see there might be a BMW in my future.

"What do you think, Sprout? Would you like to ride in a new BMW?"

She wagged her furry little tail in response. That would be something for the two of us to look forward to. I'd miss her between now and then, and I knew she'd miss me. Maybe she was the only one.

CHAPTER FIVE

"Attention, please, we will soon begin our descent into the Charles de Gaulle Airport in Paris," the voice on the intercom announced.

I stretched my legs and yawned. The combination of a first-class seat and the little pill my mother had given me had allowed me to sleep for a fair part of the trip. I looked at my watch. It said eleven in the morning, which meant it was actually more like seven in the evening, Paris time. There would hopefully still be a few shops open and I could convince the Child Save person who was meeting my flight to take me shopping.

I picked up my purse. My father had given me enough money to buy whatever I wanted or needed. He'd said he didn't want to send me halfway around the world without the benefit of enough money to deal with anything that might possibly happen, and he'd stuffed the wad of money into my hand just before we said our goodbyes. I hadn't counted it, but it felt like a thousand dollars or more. He did that all the time, usually so my mother could see but couldn't really object. It was all part of the game they played to see which of them was the *good* parent. As the referee and major beneficiary, I could hardly complain.

It had been a tearful goodbye. At least for my mother. She had really cried, but that was hardly a surprise. These days she seemed to bawl when she saw somebody win on *The Price Is Right*. I was starting to think that maybe she needed to find herself a new shrink, because the psychiatrist she was seeing obviously wasn't making her any happier.

Now my father, on the other hand—since the divorce he seemed way happier. Maybe it was because he was free to spend all of his time on his business—which is basically what he did when they were still married, but now there was no one to bug him about it. With all that extra time he was making even more money, and he used some of it to make up for not being around, or to get over feeling guilty about the divorce, or whatever. I didn't really care about the reason as long as the cash flowed my way.

Sometimes, though, he could be too busy. He'd been so obsessed with a business deal that he almost hadn't made it to the airport to see me off. And that would have been tragic. How would I have told him about Olivia's car? If I hadn't seen him, I was going to maybe come home to a Mustang. He'd hinted around about a Mercedes. I'd hinted around about a sports model, something in white. White went with practically everything. It was sad when an outfit clashed with your car.

I slipped on my shoes. I'd just go into the washroom to freshen up my makeup. I wanted to make the best impression possible. Just as I made that decision, though, the seat-belt light came on and I had to stay in my seat. I hated to be told to do anything by anybody, but it particularly irked me to be commanded by a little overhead light. I could just get up and ignore it . . . no, that wouldn't be possible with the flight attendant hovering around me. One of the things about first class was that the attendants were never far away. She'd been friendly enough throughout the flight, but she was a little past her best-before date. I could imagine doing something like her job as a bit of a lark for a while, but she had to be in her mid-thirties, for heaven's sake. She was wearing a wedding band and a tiny, tiny engagement ring. Obviously she hadn't married for money. That made it so much more painful when the marriage ended, because you didn't have a golden parachute to ease the fall.

I pulled a little mirror out of my purse. Since the worst hour of my life in that cell I swore I'd never go anywhere without a mirror again. The memory of it made me shudder—I knew I'd never stop thinking about being there. It was so real, but at the same time so unreal. It was almost dreamlike . . . no, nightmarish! I understood that some people had to go to jail, but not people like *me,* not people that *I* knew. Thank goodness my father had the money to make this work. Jail was for people who didn't have connections, power, or money.

Carefully I looked into the mirror. My eyes were still perfect. I did have nice eyes, and I'd spent enough time experimenting with the right shading—and, of course, the best makeup money could buy—to make them look even better.

I touched a finger against a little pimple that was just starting. It was barely visible, hidden beneath a layer of concealer.

If only I could have concealed my nose. I looked carefully, slowly, turning my head slightly from side to side to

see it all. There was a lot to see. It was too thick through
the bridge and there was a slight tilt and the left nostril was
definitely bigger than the right. My parents and my friends
told me there was no difference, that it was a perfect nose.
But they *would* say that. It was so obvious, as obvious as the
nose on my face. Still, there was nothing I could do about
it. At least not yet. My mother had promised me that when
I turned eighteen, if I still wasn't happy, I could have a little *alteration,* nothing drastic. I'd just have to wait. I folded
up the mirror and put it away.

The plane continued its descent and I could feel the
pressure building in my ears. The flight attendant took a
seat and put on her belt. I looked out the window. It was so
cloudy that I couldn't see the ground below. I just hoped it
wasn't raining. I'd been thinking about sitting at a little
sidewalk café and sipping a latte, watching the people parade
by. I loved watching people. It was late by American standards but this was Europe! People would still be going out,
having a trendy late supper, having a glass of wine, and
watching the world stroll by.

Then later, or maybe the next day, I could squeeze in a
bit of shopping. There were so many darling little shops in
Paris. My plan was to come home with something so new
and *off the hook* that even all those *been there, done that* kids at
my school would drool with envy. Ideally it would be something that would go with a white Mercedes convertible.

I'd been to Paris before but not without my parents.
This was going to be different! Of course there'd be
some person from Child Save to meet me at the airport
and escort me around—sort of like having your own
personal driver and tour guide—but I was sure I could
persuade them to do what I wanted. I was very good at
getting my own way. And if not, I could certainly ditch

them. I could pretend I was going to the washroom and then just accidentally wander off on my own. I had lots of money in my purse and I could speak enough French to get a taxi, order a meal, or make a purchase. Come to think of it, I could probably *live* in Paris without learning more than that! And if anybody got angry I'd just blame *them,* tell them how frightened I'd been and how irresponsible it had been for them to *lose* me. I could either threaten to sue them or squeeze out a few tears, if necessary. In the end, they'd be the ones feeling bad and guilty. If I worked it right, I might even get them to apologize to me.

The plane dropped down through the clouds and broke into open sky. Paris was blazingly bright—the City of Lights! The Eiffel Tower was all glittering with a million little lights strobing on and off. This was the sort of city I deserved! L.A. was nice and Beverly Hills was definitely my style, but there was just something so . . . so . . . *me* about Paris.

The ground got closer and closer. I closed my eyes and put my hands together and I said a little prayer: *Let the plane land safely, make sure I'm all right and safe, okay, God?* The wheels hit with a thud and my eyes popped open. We whizzed along the runway and the engines roared as the pilot worked to slow us down until the plane was just rolling smoothly. I closed my eyes again and said, *Thank you.* Not so anyone would notice. I always tried to be subtle. It would be embarrassing for anybody to see me saying a prayer.

There was a tap on my shoulder and I opened my eyes. It was the flight attendant.

"Alexandria?"

"Yes."

"We received a radio transmission. You're to disembark first. There'll be an attendant waiting at the end of the gangway. You have to be escorted directly to your connecting flight to Nairobi."

"But I wanted to shop in Paris!" I complained.

"Unless you're shopping for a Coke at one of the vending machines along the way, I think you're out of luck."

Very funny. Old, with a puny diamond, and a bad sense of humour.

"You must be very excited."

"About what?" I asked.

"You're going to Africa! Are you visiting family or is it just a pleasure trip?"

"I'm going to be doing some work. Charity work, with orphans and such."

"Good for you!" she exclaimed. "If you don't mind my asking, how old are you?"

"Sixteen . . . in four weeks."

"When I was your age all I was interested in was makeup, gossip, and boys."

I was with her on the first two, but I had little interest in boys—young men, perhaps, but certainly not *boys*.

"You must be a very good person," she said.

"Well . . ."

"I'm sorry. I didn't mean to embarrass you. My girls are still young but I hope that someday they can be like you. I'm sorry they aren't here to meet you. Your parents must be very proud of you."

I didn't answer. I didn't know what to answer. I knew they couldn't be proud of what I'd done to get here, but I thought maybe they were proud of me. No, I was *sure* they were—although right then I couldn't really think of anything I'd ever done to make them proud.

The plane came to a full and complete stop at the terminal and the seatbelt light flickered off. It was time to go.

—

I startled awake as my head bumped against the window ledge, and for a split second I panicked, not knowing where I was, until the whole airplane thing came back to me. I'd done that half a dozen times. Too long in these two planes, crossing too many time zones.

I pushed up the window shade and peered out. Nothing but complete and utter darkness. I knew we were somewhere over Africa, but where was anybody's guess. I clicked on the overhead light to see the time. My watch said nine-thirty in the evening. I'd been in the air for close to sixteen hours. We'd passed through seven time zones so that meant it was really four-thirty in the morning. My ticket said arrival was at five, so we were just half an hour away.

The plane banked sharply and I looked out the window. Suddenly the darkness below opened up, pierced by hundreds, no, thousands of little pinpricks of light. Something was down there. Something big.

Coming into Paris—the centre of the fashion world—I'd been worried about my hair and makeup. Coming into Nairobi, I wasn't as concerned. Actually, after another eight hours in a plane I just didn't have the energy to care. But what did it matter? It wasn't like I was going to run into somebody I knew. I didn't even know anybody who had ever been to Africa. It wasn't Paris, or Cannes, or London, or the Caribbean—any of those would have been different. It wasn't even Las Vegas, which was so tacky it was cool.

The wheels of the plane bounced down. Welcome to Africa.

CHAPTER SIX

One by one people claimed their baggage as it bumped along the conveyor belt. Almost everybody had already claimed their suitcases and left. Where were mine? Where were my clothes? Only a few other people from the flight were still waiting. It wasn't like I was in any danger of being left alone, though. All around me stood men, staring, watching, waiting—for what? And why did so many of them seem to be staring at *me?* I was used to being noticed, but I didn't like the way they were looking.

Another bag appeared—not mine—and the only other female standing there claimed it and left. Now it was just me, two other male passengers, and all those men. I had my carry-on bag over my shoulder, and I clutched my purse close to my chest. It held my passport, all my money, and my contact numbers. I couldn't afford to have anybody steal it.

I suddenly felt very alone. My parents weren't there. My father wasn't there to take care of me or my mother to comfort me. They weren't anywhere within five thousand miles. I was halfway around the world, waiting for my luggage, and somebody I'd never seen was going to meet me. Where were they, anyway? It wasn't right to just leave me there all alone. That person should have been waiting when the door to the plane opened.

I started to feel a bit panicky. And why was it so stuffy? I was having trouble drawing air into my lungs and I felt hot all over and . . . my goodness, I knew what was happening. It was a panic attack! I'd seen my mother go through enough of those to know what they looked like from the outside. This had to be what it felt like from the inside!

My mind raced, trying to remember what she always did when an attack hit. It was something about taking slow, deep breaths, thinking about being in a happy place, and taking a little white pill that dissolved under her tongue— that little pill I'd taken to fall asleep on the flight to Paris! I didn't have another pill, and my happy place was anywhere but here, with all those men standing around!

Maybe I could just leave, go and find a policeman. No, I couldn't abandon my luggage. Nobody was going to chase me away from my new wardrobe. I didn't care how those men looked or how they looked at me, those clothes were *mine!*

"You must be Alexandria."

I turned around. It was a woman! She was blond, young, a few years older than me, and she had a big smile. I felt so happy to see her that I had to fight the urge to wrap my arms around her, or jump up and down, or even burst into tears of happiness. Instead I scowled at her.

"You are Alexandria Hyatt, aren't you?"

"Yes. And who, may I ask, are you?" I asked.

"I'm Renée, your contact. I'm here to pick you up."

"Do you have any I.D.?"

"What?"

"I.D. Identification. I need to know you are who you say you are."

"I'm definitely me and—and I'm definitely from Child Save," she said, stammering over the words. "I will be your supervisor on this mission."

"You *say* that's who you are, but how do I know that? I need proof."

She didn't answer right away. That was either a good sign or a bad sign. She had a rather stunned look on her face. Perhaps that was her natural look.

"I have to admit that I don't have identification on me. Nobody has ever asked me for I.D. before."

"Well, I can't be responsible for the safety of others, or what they choose to ask or not ask for."

"But if you think about it," she said, "if I weren't who I say I am, how would I know that your name is Alexandria Hyatt and you're here with Child Save?"

"There might be many ways," I said. "Perhaps you got my name from the airlines."

"I guess that is a possibility. Is that your bag?"

I turned around. A large, brilliant pink suitcase had just been spat out and was making its way toward us on the conveyor belt.

"Yes, that's *one* of my bags."

"How many do you have?"

"Three, plus my carry-on, and, of course, my purse."

Two more pieces of my matching luggage appeared and rolled toward us. She helped me pull the bags off the belt.

"I don't think I've ever seen such bright luggage . . . or so *much* luggage."

"This? Is this a lot? Because I had to leave *so much* behind that I simply needed to take. Now, getting back to identification."

"As I said, I don't have any, so I guess there's only one thing to do," she said.

"And that is?"

"Since I can't convince you to come without identification, I'll just have to go and get some. I'll be back . . . in about four, maybe five hours. You sit tight. Keep an eye on your luggage. And whatever you do, don't go anywhere with anybody . . . especially those men standing by the wall over there. They are *not* your official welcoming committee."

Wait a minute—what did *that* mean? But she just turned and started to walk away. My chin dropped to the ground. She kept walking. She wasn't stopping. She wasn't even looking back!

"Wait!" I screamed.

She stopped then and turned around. I grabbed one bag and piled a second on top, pulled out the handles and awkwardly dragged, carried, and rolled the three suitcases along, bumping them off my leg as I muscled them forward. She just stood there watching, and was she . . . *smirking?*

"You can't just leave me here!" I snapped.

"I also can't physically drag you away. I'd be surprised if I could even drag your *luggage* away. Either you're coming or you're not. Yes or no?"

That smirk seemed to grow wider and more distinct. She was enjoying this. Well, I wasn't going to give her the satisfaction of hearing me beg her to—

"I guess that means no." She turned around and started to walk away again.

"I'm coming!" I yelled out, and she stopped one more time. "I need some help with my luggage," I said.

"So, what's the magic word?"

Magic word? Abracadabra? *Voilà*? What was she talking about?

"Please," she said.

"Please?"

"Now that didn't take much, did it?"

She grabbed two of the wheeled bags and I followed behind with the rest of my things. I scrambled to keep up with her, my heels clicking against the hard floor. It was hard to move quickly in heels. My father had suggested that I wear running shoes, but I'd told him I wasn't planning on entering a race.

I fell in beside her. "I'm really looking forward to a long, hot bath, but first I should have a little nap."

"A nap you can have in the truck, but the hot bath might be a slightly longer wait."

"I can wait."

"Good. Patience is a virtue."

"Yeah, right," I mumbled under my breath.

"Did you say something?"

"Nothing . . . nothing at all. How long before I can take a bath?"

"Three weeks. We don't have any bathtubs at the centre. Just showers."

I hated showers. They were just so . . . gym class. "A shower it will have to be."

"Either that or stay dirty, your choice."

I had just met this person but I was certain that I didn't like her. I was a very good judge of people and I could size them up almost instantly. She was not the type of person that I'd even *consider* having as a friend. For starters, I could hardly imagine being friends with anybody who wore socks and sandals together! Didn't this woman have

a full-length mirror in her house? If she did, she would
have known what that looked like. She might as well have
worn a sign that said "Loser." And of all people, *she* was
going to be my supervisor. If I didn't do what she said, I
could end up in juvenile detention after all. Did that suck
or what?

She stopped beside a gigantic truck. It looked like a
garbage truck. Why would she stop there?

"Here, I'll take that," a man said as he stepped out of
the darkness.

I was stunned.

"Let me have your bag," he said. He was almost as
black as the night and he was wearing a red dress and a
blanket! I was being robbed by a weird African transvestite!

When he stepped toward me and reached out his
hand, I swung my purse and struck him square in the face!
He wasn't getting *my* wardrobe without a fight! He staggered backward and I swung the purse again, screaming as
loudly as I could to get attention!

"What are you doing?" Renée yelled.

I pointed at the man. He'd backed off a couple of
steps. Just to emphasize my point I screamed again, louder
and longer.

"This is Nebala," Renée said. "He's with us."

I stopped mid-scream and mid-swing. He smiled.
Brilliant white teeth stood out in contrast to the black of
his face.

"He's not a mugger?" I asked meekly.

"He's our guide and guard. He was just trying to help
you with your luggage. Let me introduce you."

He reached out his hand and reluctantly I did the same.

"Nebala," he said, and his smile widened.

"Alexandria Hyatt."

"Nebala, could you please put her bags in the back?" Renée asked.

I suppose I should have guessed that he was there to take care of me. For the amount of money my father had paid for this trip, I expected a little more service.

He grabbed the big bag and with one hand lifted it up and over his head, as if it were empty. I knew just how much it did weigh because my father had to pay extra charges for it. With the other hand he scaled a ladder on the side of the truck, and he tossed my bag up and away into the back. He jumped down like a big cat, hitting the pavement without making a sound. He picked up the other two remaining bags, putting the smaller of the two under his arm, and scaled the side of the truck again.

"If there were a lot of people you'd have to ride in the back too," Renée said, "but since there are only three of us we can all ride in the cab."

She reached up and opened the door to the cab. I went to climb in and then stopped. This was the driver's side of the vehicle, and I wasn't planning on driving.

"Just climb up and slide over into the middle," Renée said.

Okay, that made sense. I climbed up. The steering wheel was on the wrong side of the truck! Renée climbed in beside me and Nebala got in the other side, settling in beside the steering wheel.

"The steering wheel," I muttered, "it's . . . it's on the wrong side of the truck."

Nebala looked at me and then at the wheel. He shook his head. "No, this is the side where I left it."

Renée broke into laughter, startling me.

"That side," Nebala said, pointing to where Renée sat, "would be the wrong side."

"Kenya follows the British model," Renée explained. "They drive on the left side of the road."

I'd been to London and knew that the British drove on the *wrong* side of the road, but I didn't know about Kenya. I thought it was just a thing in England because they wanted to be different, sort of like bad teeth, pale skin, and lousy cuisine.

"I don't care which side we drive on, as long as we drive. Can I have that shower as soon as—"

The truck started and the rumbling of the engine overwhelmed my words.

"—as soon as we get there?" I said, finishing the sentence.

"You can, although you might want to have something to eat before your shower. That way you could meet everybody."

I most certainly didn't want to meet anybody until I'd showered, and done my hair, and reapplied my makeup. You never get a second chance to make a good first impression.

"Maybe I should wait until later to meet them. I'm really not a morning person."

"What a shock!" she said. Was she being sarcastic?

"And I'm not hungry," I said.

"You might be by the time we get there, although by then lunch will probably already be over."

I wasn't that hungry so it didn't matter that much and . . . did she say *lunch?* The sun was just coming up.

"You mean breakfast, not lunch," I said. And I was the one who hadn't slept! The truck hit a gigantic bump and we were all thrown into the air before bouncing back onto the bench seat.

"No," Renée said. "Breakfast will be long gone before we arrive. Lunch is what I'm aiming for."

Either these people ate breakfast in the middle of the night or something was seriously strange. "When do you eat lunch here?"

"Noon. Twelve or so."

"But it's only . . . only . . ." I looked at my watch and tried to rotate the hour hand to tell me the time. "It's only six-thirty."

"That's what I mean. It's going to be around a six-hour drive to get to the compound."

"What? Six hours? Is it on the other side of the country?"

"About a hundred and fifty miles. That's how long it will take on these roads."

"And these roads aren't bad," Nebala added. "At least, compared to some others. When the rainy season hits this drive can take twice as long."

"I'm not driving in this thing for six hours. I simply refuse to do that!"

Renée looked at me and then at Nebala. "Okay, stop the truck."

The gears ground down, the engine whirred, and he pulled the truck off to the side of the road—the *wrong* side of the road.

"Alexandria, I know you're tired," she said.

"I'm *exhausted!*"

"Okay, exhausted. You are also probably hungry, thirsty, confused, jet-lagged, and at least a little angry that you're here to begin with."

"A little angry? Hah!"

"Okay, maybe a lot angry. Regardless, I'm not prepared to spend six hours with you in this truck listening to you complain. So, you have three options. One, you go in the back with the luggage."

"You can't be serious."

"Very. Two," she said, "you get out and walk."

I looked out through the windshield. It was now light enough to see. There were cars and trucks and motorcycles careening along the road. The way they were moving reminded me more of bumper cars at the circus than any roadway I'd ever seen. All along the roads, on both sides, was a steady stream of people walking. Each and every person was black—black and foreign and Kenyan. There was no way she could possible leave me at the side of the road.

"And the third option is that you just stop complaining and accept that you don't always get what you want."

"Mick Jagger," I said.

"What?"

"Nothing." Maybe *she* didn't usually get what she wanted, but *I* did.

"Well?" she asked.

I looked straight ahead. "Option three." As far as I was concerned, I'd be happy not to say another word to anybody for the next three weeks.

CHAPTER SEVEN

I was so tired that I was starting to feel nauseous, but every time I drifted off I was rudely awoken by another enormous bump in the road. This had to be, without a doubt, the worst road in the entire world and the worst ride of my entire life.

Feeling bored, I looked out the window. I saw the same things I'd been seeing for hours: rutted, rotten, red roadway winding off into the distance. On both sides of the road was scrubby growth—not jungle, but certainly not *Lion King* country, either. Little clusters of buildings— no, shacks—appeared from time to time at the side of the road. These were stores, apparently. For the first time in my life I'd discovered stores that even *I* didn't want to shop in. And while there were very few vehicles, there were always people. They'd be sitting in the shade, or standing in groups, and lots and lots of people just walked along the side of the road. Didn't these people have better things to do than wait or walk?

Along with the people was a strange mixture of animals: cows, goats, chickens, donkeys. They were in the fields, scratching at the dirt in front of the stores, by the road, and on the road. Nebala would bounce the truck forward and at the last minute the cow or goat or donkey would just move aside. He never slowed down for them or swerved, but he never hit any of them. They just got out of his way. Smart animals. I guess the stupid ones had been killed a long time ago. Sort of like Darwin's theory of evolution, but with cars and cows.

The few vehicles we did see were just as likely to be off at the side of the road. Somebody would be working on a flat tire, or something underneath the hood, or the vehicle itself. And those that were driving were either moving slowly or dodging back and forth all over the road trying to avoid the gullies. Sometimes we'd be passed by these little minivan things. They had bundles on the roof and what seemed like dozens and dozens of people crammed inside. Renée called them *matatus*, and they were apparently famous for both overloading and under-driving. They were, I guess, like taxicabs everywhere. Probably the drivers spoke as much English as the cab drivers in New York City or L.A.

Almost every time we did pass a vehicle, Nebala would wave and the other driver would wave back. Sometimes the vehicles would come to a stop, driver to driver. They'd yell out something or, if they were close enough, even extend their arms so they could shake. Either this guy knew everybody in Kenya or these were the friendliest people in the world.

The first couple of times we stopped for him to have a conversation I tried to listen in, but there was no point, really. Whatever language they were speaking was different from any language I'd ever heard. Nebala obviously spoke

it, but Renée could chatter a bit, as well. She'd nod her
head in agreement and throw out a sentence or two during
the conversations.

It struck me as strange that they weren't simply speaking English. Why didn't everybody just give up all those
other, foreign languages like they were last year's fashions?
Wouldn't the whole world be a better place if everybody
spoke English? Wouldn't that *Change The World*? Because
that's what was written across Renée's T-shirt. Frankly, if
I'd been her I would have started the whole *change* thing
with a better T-shirt. Who went around with slogans on
their clothing like they were some sort of walking bumper
sticker or billboard? I didn't want any writing on my
clothing unless it said "Gucci."

To be honest, though, the T-shirt—her brown T-shirt—
kind of matched the rest of her outfit. Maybe "matched"
wasn't the right word, because nothing really matched, but
it did fit the pattern. She was such a fashion disaster—a
walking, breathing fashion train wreck. She could have
been the poster child for a new season of *What Not to Wear*.
Brown shirt, blue safari shorts, red socks and black sandals,
and a gold bandana tied around her head. Was she colour
blind as well as fashion blind? Or maybe she'd had to get
up so early to get me this morning that she'd dressed in the
dark. Even then, what were the odds of getting every sin-
gle colour to turn out differently? Either she had been shot
in the head by a strange kind of Russian roulette for clothing, or this was some type of deliberate attempt to look
hideous.

I knew some girls like that. They knew they didn't have
the looks to compete so they just didn't try. I didn't know
whether they were to be admired for at least acknowledg-
ing the truth, or pitied, or both. But the thing was, Renée

could have been a player. She wasn't wearing any makeup but she had very nice skin, good bone structure, nice eyes, and a nose that was smaller than mine. She was a bit on the short side—certainly there was no danger of her becoming a runway model—but she was relatively well proportioned. Losing a few pounds wouldn't have hurt, but who couldn't say that? Thirty minutes with my makeup case, some flattering clothes, and some tweezers—those eyebrows needed some serious work—and I could have lifted her a few pegs up the food chain. Who knows, she might even have managed to get a ring on that empty wedding finger. Probably nothing big or expensive, but a ring, nevertheless.

I guess some people would have called her a natural beauty, but I really didn't believe in that idea. I saw beauty as the end product of a complicated process involving skin care, makeup, clothes, lighting, and often some surgical enhancement. It was natural to want to look beautiful, but nature was only a bit player in the process. Given enough time, money, diet, exercise, clothes, a good stylist, and a first-rate surgeon and anybody could look right at home on Venice Beach.

Instantly my hand came up to the bridge of my nose. If rubbing it could have worn it down I wouldn't have needed to consider surgery.

We slowed down again and Nebala brought the truck to a stop right beside another truck, which had been travelling the other way. He and the other driver got into a long and loud discussion, with lots of laughter.

I didn't understand much, but what I had been able to figure out was that the word *"jambo"* probably meant "hello," or some variation on "hello," and *"kwaheri"* was "goodbye." And I wasn't 100 percent sure but the word *"asante"* was used a lot and it might have been "please" or "thank you" or "you're welcome." If I could just have figured out how to say "toilet," "sparkling water," and, "yes, I'll purchase that," I'd have been all set. Although from what I'd seen of Kenya so far there was nothing I'd actually have wanted to purchase. I don't know who would have been more shocked by that, my mother or my father. My mother loved shopping even more than I did. In fact, if my family had lived in Kenya my parents might still have been married. It would have eliminated half the arguments they had about her spending money and overextending her credit cards. Dust, mud, and cows were never big on her list of things to buy.

We started up again—everybody yelled out *"Kwaheri"*— and almost instantly we hit a humungous pothole and I was bounced so hard that I nearly hit the roof of the truck.

"Could you try to miss *some* of the bumps?" I snapped angrily.

"Miss them?" he questioned. "You mean I'm *not* supposed to try to hit them?"

Renée cackled like a bird at his lame attempt at humour. Then she jabbered at him in that stupid little language they spoke, and he threw back his head and howled as well.

I almost asked what she had said, because I was positive that it was about me, but I was equally positive that they weren't about to tell me. Well, let them make their stupid little jokes. In three weeks she'd still be some two-bit tour guide eating road dust, and he'd be some guy wearing a red dress and a blanket driving a beat-up old truck. He looked like some drag queen trucker.

We hit another bump and again I shot up into the air.

"Sorry," he said, "*miss* them . . . not *hit* them . . . *miss* them . . . I'll try to remember."

This was a new low. I was getting sarcasm and attitude from some guy in a crazy get-up.

CHAPTER EIGHT

"We're almost there," Renée said.

I peered hard through the windshield, but I didn't see any *there* there. We were on a bumpy little stretch of road that looked like every other stretch of road we'd passed for the past hour. Maybe the road was a little narrower and less rutted, but it all looked pretty much the same.

We turned a corner and a large green metal gate stood in our way. Stretched out in both directions were strands of wire making a high fence, and on it were large signs that read, "Danger! Hatari! Electric Fence!" Did "*hatari*" mean danger?

The truck ground to a stop right in front of the gate and Nebala blasted the horn. Two men dressed in identical lime-green jumpsuits came running toward the gate and started to open it.

"What are we doing here?" I demanded. "Why are we going in?"

"This is our destination."

I felt my whole body flush. Had this whole thing been nothing more than a gigantic scam to put me in jail on the other side of the world, where my father and my lawyer couldn't help me?

"This isn't part of the arrangement!" I screamed. "I'm supposed to go to a program! I'm not supposed to go to jail!"

Both Renée and Nebala laughed. This wasn't funny!

"This isn't jail," Renée said. "This is paradise!"

"Since when does paradise need an electric fence to keep people in?" I demanded.

"It's not to keep people in so much as to keep the outside out. Don't worry," she said as she patted me on the leg.

"Don't touch me!" I snapped, and brushed her hand away.

She was visibly startled. "I'm sorry. I was just trying to reassure you."

"I don't need your reassurance," I lied. And if that was the best reassurance she could give me, it was pretty useless anyway.

The truck bumped forward and through the gates. I looked over and in the side mirror I could see the two guards close the gate behind us.

"You'll see, there's nothing to be afraid of," Renée said.

"I'm not afraid," I responded instinctively, although the quaver in my voice might have given me away.

The truck came to a stop, and as Renée opened the door I practically pushed her out in my rush to get away.

"You can't keep me here in this jail!"

"It's *not* a jail."

"And I suppose those two aren't guards? And that isn't a locked gate and an electrified fence?"

"Those are guards—we call them *askari*—but they're here to protect you."

"Hah! They're here to keep me imprisoned behind your fence!"

Renée didn't answer. Instead she got that smirky look that had already become familiar and annoying. She turned toward the guards and yelled something I didn't understand. They both nodded, and one unlocked the chain holding the gate shut and swung it open.

"Please feel free to go out, if you wish," she said. She bowed and gestured toward the gate.

"Go where?"

"Wherever you wish. This is not a prison. But I have to warn you of the dangers out there."

"Dangers?" I scoffed. "I've been in some pretty dangerous places before." Once, when I was twelve, I'd got separated from my parents and ended up walking through downtown L.A. all by myself—not the shopping part, but the places where nobody speaks English and the street gangs hang out. It was the scariest fifteen minutes of my life.

"Well, in that case I'm sure you wouldn't have any trouble with a leopard or an elephant or a lion."

"Yeah, like those are around here."

"Alexandria, we're in Africa. Where is it that you think elephants and lions live?" Renée asked. "That's why the fence is electrified. That's the only way to stop an elephant."

"Here," Nebala said. He pulled a wooden club from under his belt. "This is a *konga*. You can use it against a leopard."

I drew my hands back, refusing to take it. "I've got something more powerful than that." I opened my purse and pulled out my cellphone, holding it aloft like a weapon. "I'm going to call both my father and my lawyer. You two are in *such* trouble!"

"Again, feel free."

I flipped the phone open and it started searching for a network to connect. It continued to search and search and search but it was finding nothing.

"You can't stop me from calling my lawyer. I know my rights!"

"Nobody is stopping you except nature, the laws of physics, and a complete absence of cellphone towers in this valley. Even *you* can't defy the laws of nature, Alexandria." Renée paused. "But you see through those trees, in the distance? I know you can get reception from the top of that hill. Right, Nebala?"

He pulled back his blanket. Beside the *konga* was a long, sheathed knife, and beside that was a cellphone! He took the phone off the belt and held it to his ear.

"Can you hear me now?" he asked.

Renée burst into laughter. I finally figured out where I'd heard that laugh before—in *The Wizard of Oz,* the Wicked Witch of the West!

"Up there you can get reception," Nebala said.

"If you can get past the animals, you can make a call."

"And don't forget the snakes," Nebala added.

"There are snakes?"

"Pythons, adders, black mambas, and spitting cobras," he said.

Renée shuddered. "I hate those the most. They really freak me out." She turned directly to me. "Do you know about spitting cobras?"

I shook my head.

"They basically spray venom in the form of misty droplets. It can travel up to two yards. It causes permanent blindness if it isn't treated."

"How do you treat it?"

"You wash out your eyes," Renée said.

Nebala nodded. "With milk or urine."

"Urine? You mean *pee?*"

He nodded again.

"That is just totally disgusting. Why would you even think of using urine if you could use milk?"

"Milk may be hard to find. Pee is always available."

"I'd rather *die* than rub pee in my eyes!"

"Interestingly, that's basically the choice," Renée said. "Wash out your eyes or die. Once you're wounded and can't get away then the snake bites you and injects venom directly into your bloodstream."

"Dead, pretty quick," Nebala added.

"How quick?"

"Depends. On the size of the snake, how much venom has been stored since it last struck, and the body weight of the victim."

"How much do you weigh?" Renée asked.

"About one-fifteen," I said, lying off the last seven pounds I needed to lose.

"That's awfully light for your height."

Said like somebody who was extremely jealous. Envy, straight envy.

"At your weight you'd probably be dead in about two hours. But those sunglasses of yours would probably protect you anyway and you wouldn't need to wash your eyes out. Just try not to surprise one. They generally strike only when they're startled."

"Walk like this," Nebala said. He made exaggerated

steps, landing very heavily. "They need to feel the vibra-
tions so they can get away."

*Or feel them so they know where you are and come looking
for you,* I thought. Wasn't it best not to let the snake know
you were around so it wouldn't spit at you?

"Look, Alexandria, for better or worse you are going
no place right now. Later today if you want to make that
call I'll ask Nebala to bring you up to the top. Right now,
let's just get some lunch."

I *was* hungry.

"And you'll have a chance to meet our other guests,"
she said.

"Guests—is that the word you're using to describe
your prisoners?"

"There are no prisoners here."

"Fine. How many people are here who are being
forced to be here?"

Renée held up one finger.

"One other?"

She shook her head. "Just one. You. Doesn't that make
you feel special?"

I *was* special. "Just how many people are here?"

"Twenty."

"But if they're not being forced to be here, why are
they here?" I asked.

"I'll let them tell you their stories themselves," Renée
said, and I followed her into the compound. Really, what
choice did I have?

CHAPTER NINE

Defeated once again, I followed Renée along a little cobblestone path. I was sure they were just trying to scare me with that snake business, but whatever, I was still going to stay on the path and walk heavy. Hundreds of dance lessons instantly washed away and replaced with a walk like a Neanderthal.

I heard voices and laughter and singing before I saw anybody. We rounded a corner and there were people seated under a large thatched roof. There were tables, and a big fireplace was set into the one wall of the building. It was some sort of outdoor dining room.

I did a quick count: twenty-three people. A few of them were older so they were probably the staff. A few more females than males. They were so busy that they didn't seem to notice us. They all wore T-shirts and shorts and sandals. The girls all seemed to have their hair in ponytails or tied back with bandanas. Apparently, here Renée was a fashion icon.

"Renée!" somebody shouted, and everybody stopped talking and yelled out greetings. A bunch of kids jumped to their feet and rushed over, and she was enveloped in a group hug. I moved off to the side to make sure I wasn't caught up in it.

"Hello!" a girl said to me. "I'm Andrea, but my friends call me Andy!"

"Yes, hello." I assumed I'd be calling her Andrea. Perhaps if she put on a little makeup and did something with her hair they might actually realize that she was a girl and not a boy named Andy.

"Everybody!" Renée yelled out. "I'd like you to meet Alexandria!"

There was a roar of yells and greetings and they started to rush toward me. If anybody even tried to hug me I'd hit them with my—first Andrea and then two other girls wrapped their arms around me! Didn't these people know anything about personal space? I tried to break free but a few other kids joined in and I was trapped in the middle . . . in the middle of a group hug . . . how disgusting was this? And somebody, or more than one person, had some serious need for deodorant.

This was all awful. It had been bad enough when I'd thought I was entering a jail. Now it felt more like a cult— a cult that had *absolutely* no style. If you were going to blindly follow somebody, at least make sure that they were somebody named Dolce or Gabbana.

Renée rescued me from the crush and introduced me to the other staff. There was a Jessie, a Robin, an Alex, and a Dave. Cute. Everybody had a cute little name, and they all pretended to be so friendly and happy to meet me. I wasn't there to pretend.

"We're going to have everybody introduce themselves

and say a few words about why they're here," Renée announced. "Let's start with our newest guest, Alexandria."

My eyes widened. I knew what she trying to do, make me look stupid by giving me no notice. It wasn't going to work. Public speaking was just about having confidence in yourself, and I had even more of that than I had money.

"As you know, my name is Alexandria . . . Alexandria *Hyatt.*" I said the name clearly. In Brentwood my last name was known. They didn't look as though they recognized it. "I'm almost sixteen. I live in Brentwood, California. My favourite colour is taupe, although aquamarine matches my eyes perfectly. I don't know what else to say."

"Why are you here?" a girl asked.

"I really didn't have any choice. I had to come," I said without thinking. Now I was thinking: if I was the only one who had been ordered to come here by the courts, maybe I shouldn't have told everybody.

"I had no choice either," a boy said.

Huh? But I'd thought I was the only one who had been forced to come. Had Renée lied to me?

"When I found out about the needs of the people," he continued, "I knew I *had* to come here."

Others kids started clapping and hooting. I knew we weren't talking about the same thing, but I wasn't going to say anything to correct it. Let them believe what they wanted. What did I care? It wasn't like I knew any of them or would ever see them again once my sentence had been served.

"Now that we know a little about Alexandria, who'd like to share their story with her?" Renée asked.

A dozen hands shot up into the air.

"Sarah, why don't you start?"

"Hello, my name is Sarah, and I'm from Boise, Idaho, and I'm here as part of a group from my church."

"Could all the members of the group stand up, please?" Renée said.

Nine other people got to their feet. There were four guys and five other girls. The guys had short hair and the girls wore sensible shoes. They all had that look, that . . . *church* look. Apparently, I *had* wandered into a cult.

"We had a speaker from Child Save come and speak to our youth group. We learned about children who had no fresh water or schools to go to, and we decided that since we had so much, and they had so little, we wanted to help. We raised almost twenty thousand dollars to help build a school."

Everybody started clapping and cheering. Of course I just clapped along.

"And then," Sarah continued, "we raised funds to have ten of us come here to do the actual building and to meet the children we were helping." There was some more clapping as she sat down.

The other members of the youth group took turns introducing themselves. They all shared a bland sameness, and the names all blurred together. There was a Kelly and two Taylors—one a boy and one a girl—and a Todd, Tim, Jimmy, and two Britneys. Tim I might actually remember. Give him a better haircut—he looked like his parents still cut it—and he might have had some potential. Not that he'd be up to my dating standards, but, anyway, better.

Another girl stood up to talk. I was pretty sure she wasn't a church kid. She was older, dressed with a little more style, and her makeup wasn't half bad.

"Hello, everybody. Hello, Alex," she said, looking directly at me.

"It's Alexandria," I said coldly. Nobody except my closest friends would ever call me that, and she wasn't about to become one of them.

"Sorry. Didn't mean to offend. My name is Chris. Well, I guess really it's Christina if we really feel a need to get formal . . . or pretentious."

I bristled. Was she seriously taking me on?

"I came here to help, but also to learn, and to help prepare myself for a career in international development," she said.

That certainly sounded snooty, although I didn't know exactly what "international development" was.

"I'm in my third year of university . . . on a scholarship . . . and one of my professors felt that this experience would make me an even better student."

Would it be impolite to vomit?

"I have studied the people of this region fairly extensively and I am familiar with their culture and customs. And, of course, I can speak some Swahili."

She finished up her little speech. What I'd really learned was that she was a pain—a showoffy, pretentious, annoying pain.

The next person got up and started talking. I stayed focused on Christina as she sat down. She was clearly the best-looking girl there. At least, she was until I showed up. I should have expected that she wouldn't be pleased to have me around. It wasn't going to be easy for her to share the spotlight. Who was I fooling? With me around it wasn't about sharing. I was going to keep the whole spotlight to myself. I'd have to keep a close eye on her, though. If she was smart enough to instantly size me up as a threat to her alpha status, then she was smart enough to try to stay top dog.

Person after person stood up and talked. Different names, different faces, different voices, but the same basic story. The same basic sermon. If they were pretending to be saints for my benefit they could stop wasting their breath and my time. I was hardly listening, and what I did hear didn't impress me. At least I had an excuse. I *had* to be there. These people were so stupid that they'd made a choice. I couldn't even imagine that. Didn't they have any better place to be, things to do, or people to hang with?

One of the staff got up, thanked everybody for sharing, and then told them it was time to leave to get back to work. Everybody practically jumped to their feet. The way they were acting, all excited, you would have thought she had said get back to the *spa* instead of work. Reluctantly I got up too. My legs felt wobbly.

"You won't be going with them this afternoon," Renée said. "I think you need to unpack and rest."

I felt so grateful I almost said thank you.

"Your luggage has been brought to your tent."

I was glad I didn't have to bring it all down . . . did she say *tent?*

"Excuse me? I'm staying in a tent?"

"We call them tents, but really it isn't like you'll be camping."

"That's good, because I *don't* camp."

"It sounds like there are lots of things you don't do. Lots of limits you place on yourself. Come and see before you judge."

I trailed behind her along the path. I was tired of following her. We rounded a corner and there was a cluster of large green tents. It was easy to see which one was mine because my luggage was on the front step. The bright pink of the suitcases and forest green of the canvas looked rather striking together. I never would have placed those colours side by side, but it was something to keep in mind for the future.

We stepped up onto the wooden deck of the tent. The canvas formed a roof and there were two folding chairs sitting outside.

"The tent itself has a concrete floor and there are electrical outlets," Renée said. She opened the zipper and pulled back the canvas door. She stepped in and I followed behind and . . . wait . . . there were clothes on the bed, and they weren't *my* clothes.

"This has to be a mistake. Somebody else is already in this tent."

"Your roommate."

I gasped. "I have to share this tent with somebody?"

"Two beds. Two people."

"I *don't* share."

Renée smirked. I hated that smirk. "This is the only unoccupied bed in the whole camp, so I think that your choice, once again, is limited. Do you want to spend time discussing this further or do you want to unpack and take that shower?"

"I want to shower." Seventeen hours in the air and six more in a dusty truck had made a shower my top priority, over almost anything else imaginable.

I looked around the room. "Where is my shower?"

"Your shower is down the way in the big cement building."

I gasped again. "You aren't telling me that I have to share a shower with every other person here, are you?"

"Not everybody. Just all the girls. Two stalls for the boys and two for the girls. Common showers."

That all seemed so . . . so . . . *common*. In my whole life
I'd never had to share a bedroom, shower, or toilet. Maybe
jail would have been better. Then I remembered the stain-
less-steel toilet in the middle of the holding cell. Down
the way would be better.

I shook my head. "Right now I just don't care. I just
want to get into a hot shower and stay there for a long
time."

"You can do that now, but not in the morning."

"I can't?"

"They're shared, remember. If you're in there too long
you'll be keeping other people waiting. As well, we have a
very small water-heater, so if you take too much hot water
other people will get none. That wouldn't be fair."

Fair had nothing to do with this. Getting what I
wanted did, and there was only one way for that to happen.
I'd get up early and take the first shower. That way it was
guaranteed that I'd have hot water, even if I was the only
one who did. I just needed to know how early *early* was.

"Renée, what time do people generally get up in the
morning?" I asked sweetly.

"That depends on how long it takes for them to get
ready. Some people just splash some water in their face and
throw on some clothes."

"Yes, I've noticed," I said, wondering if she got the
shot. "But what time is breakfast and what time do we
leave?"

"Breakfast is at seven and we try to be on the road by
seven-thirty."

"No, seriously."

"Seriously."

"Do you have any idea how early that means I would
have to get up in order to be ready to leave?" I questioned.

"I'm almost afraid to ask."

"Is this negotiable?" I asked.

"Feel free to talk to the group. We try to have discussions, build consensus."

I tried not to smile. I was pretty sure I could talk this group into doing pretty well whatever I wanted. This would be no challenge.

"Although I have to warn you that this group is pretty gung-ho."

"What does that mean?"

"Enthusiastic. Yesterday they wanted to stay at the school working at the end of the day, and they were talking about getting out even earlier this morning so they could get to the school earlier and begin work."

I was struck by the terrible thought that if I brought it up I could end up leaving even earlier. Maybe I shouldn't be so confident about what I could talk them into doing. These kids were a little odd, certainly different from the people in my school and in my group. Odd kids might have odd ways of thinking.

"It would certainly be an interesting talk," Renée said.

I hated that word *interesting*. It could mean almost anything.

"I get the feeling you're a very persuasive speaker," Renée said. "I'm willing to bet that you are usually able to talk people into doing lots of things, aren't you?"

She gave me a little smile. I knew she meant that as a shot. Fine.

"Well," I said, "I guess it's like they say . . . it takes one to know one." I smiled back.

I tried to do a little mental calculation. If I laid out my clothes the night before that would save me at least fifteen minutes. I'd need an hour for hair and makeup and I was planning on at least fifteen minutes in the shower. I didn't really need to eat breakfast. Losing a little weight wouldn't be my worst African souvenir. This might be the chance for me to actually *become* one-fifteen rather than just *claiming* to be one-fifteen. That meant that to get out by seven-thirty I'd have to get up at . . . quarter to six. Okay, that was just insane! I'd been up that late but I'd never gotten up that early!

"This is really not possible. I'm warning you right now that I am really not a morning person."

"I guess that explains everything," she said.

"Do you get paid to take shots at me?" I asked.

"No, that I do for free. Have your shower and a nap and we'll see you at supper."

I sat there thinking through my morning routine. If I wanted to look my best I had no choice but to get up that early. But, really, what did I even care what these people thought? None of them had the style or the class to even know what I was doing or wearing or what I looked like. I could just sleep in and . . . no, I couldn't do that. Regardless of their lack of style, I still had standards. I still had myself to impress.

CHAPTER TEN

I tried to nap but it just wasn't happening. Instead, I was just lost in thought. All of this, everything that was happening, was so surreal that I kept playing it all over and over in my head.

I heard the zipper on the tent open. Time to meet my roommate. I sat up and—

"It's you," I said. It was that *awful* Christina person.

"It is. Very observant." She slumped down on her bed, right on top of the clothes and belongings that littered the surface.

I looked at her as she ignored me. She was covered with mud and dirt. Perfect way to climb into your bed.

"You're filthy," I said.

"And tired. But at least it's a good tired."

I wasn't sure what that even meant. "What were you doing?"

"Mainly mixing cement." She sat up and threw her legs

over the side of the bed so she was facing me. "Do you have any idea how much work is involved with mixing . . . wait, what am I saying? Of course, you wouldn't have a clue."

That was clearly meant as an insult. I took it as a compliment instead.

"I was also plastering, and I helped to put in a window. The building is almost three-quarters finished."

"Were you building a house?" I asked.

"A school. That's what we're here for . . . you knew that, right?"

"Of course I knew." Of course I had managed to block out what they'd been blathering on about earlier.

"I'd better take a shower and get changed before supper," she said. She got up, grabbed another "Change The World" T-shirt, a towel, and a little toiletry bag, and started for the door.

"How long do we have before supper?"

"About forty-five minutes."

I jumped to my feet. "Then I'd better get ready too."

She gave me a questioning look. "What else do you need to do?"

I smiled. It was too late to make a better first impression, but I wanted to be completely stunning the second time around.

"I want to touch up my makeup, and I really need to straighten my hair. This humidity is playing havoc. Do you know where I can plug in my straightener?"

"I think Nairobi would work."

"No, no, you don't understand. I want to know where I can plug it in *here* at the camp."

"No, you're the one who doesn't understand. The generator is only turned on for a few hours each night, after it gets dark."

"And this generator thing matters because . . . ?"

She gave me a Renée-like look. "The generator produces electricity, and your hair thing needs electricity to work. Unless it's battery operated."

"But that would be ridiculous."

"Not nearly as ridiculous as bringing along a hair-straightener to the middle of the Maasai Mara."

"Ridiculous is not having electricity. Everybody has electricity."

"Everybody in the world *you* come from."

Yeah, like *she* was from the middle of a desert.

"Out here it comes from a generator—for those few who are rich enough to afford one. But I guess you'd know all about being rich."

The way she said "rich" was like it was some sort of dirty word. I wasn't about to take that from her.

"I imagine to the local people we must all seem rich," I countered.

"We are. Rich beyond their wildest dreams."

"But at least some people come over because they really want to help."

"Yeah, that's true of *some* of us."

There was no mistaking that statement. She was one of the "some" who came to help and I wasn't.

"But here's a thought," I said. "How much better would it be for the people here if, instead of us coming over and doing a little bit of work, we just sent the money for our airfare instead? Can you imagine how many people would have been helped if you had simply sent your money over here instead of sending yourself? The difference would just be amazing!"

She gave me the dirtiest, coldest look imaginable, said something else under her breath, and left the tent. I had to stop myself from laughing out loud. Bonus points for me. Not only had I shut her up, I'd sent her away! But enough about her. I had something really important to worry about—my hair.

No electricity meant no curling iron, no hair-straightener, not even a blow-dryer. I could do wonders with just a blow-dryer if I had to. These people had thrown proper hair care back to the age of the dinosaur! But what could I do? Renée was right, this wasn't a prison . . . I knew that because prisons had electricity.

Despite my best efforts I was the last to arrive for supper, and almost every seat was taken. I scoped the scene. There were only two open spots. One was beside Renée and opposite to Christina—I could see why nobody wanted that spot—and the other was squarely in the middle of "Church Town." Talk about limited options. I assumed that room service was out of the question so I quickly thought it through. Sitting by Renée and Christina would show them that I wasn't afraid of them. But it might also give them the mistaken idea that I actually liked them. I'd have to risk that. I couldn't have them smelling fear.

There was only one positive to all of this. At least I could make an entrance. I straightened my scarf and then, slowly, walked into the dining area, my heels clicking against the wooden floor. I tried not to be too obvious about watching as heads started to turn my way.

"Alexandria!" one of the church girls yelled out as she got to her feet and wildly waved. She gestured to the open seat at her table.

I guess the choice was made for me. Slowly, deliberately, like I was strutting the runway, I glided across the room. No earth-shaking "snake walk" for me. I didn't need to look to know I was being observed. Any boy who wasn't looking at me had some gender confusion issues he needed to work out. Hair-straightener or no hair-straightener, I knew I looked good.

"You probably don't remember all of our names," the girl said. "I'm Sarah."

"Of course I remember you," I lied.

They went around the table once more and introduced themselves. I repeated each name in my head. That was the best way to put names with faces. And they all had perky names to go with their perky smiles. They reminded me of the Mickey Mouse Club. But then again, that was where Britney and Christina and even Justin started out before they made it big time. I'd be willing to share a pair of mouse ears with Justin any day.

I listened with one ear tuned to the conversation going on around me while still eavesdropping on what was being talked about at the next table. Different table, different people, different words, but the same attitude. These people were all seriously buzzed and wired. The whole place was like a gigantic cheerleading squad minus the matching uniforms. Although, quite frankly, there were so many "Change The World" T-shirts that it might as well have been the uniform.

Personally I thought my choice of clothing was a dozen notches above this crowd. I had on an ivory-coloured silk blouse and forest-green safari shorts. I was glad I'd gone with low heels instead of the high ones. It was a nice contrast to the sneakers and sandals worn by everybody else, but not too provocative. Maybe I should

have added the darker-green linen jacket to the whole
ensemble just to draw out the overall colour—

"Alexandria?"

I startled out of my thoughts.

"Do you want tea or coffee with supper?" Sarah asked.
She gestured over my shoulder. There was a waiter standing there holding two pots.

"Could I have a sparkling water instead?"

"Water?" he asked.

"Yes. Either Perrier or Evian would be fine."

"Tea or coffee," he repeated.

"I want—"

"I'll get it," Tim said as he bounced to his feet. Right,
Tim, the almost-acceptable candidate for a bit of harmless
flirtation. He raced across the room and returned with a
bottle of water and handed it to me.

"This is just water," I said, with a bit of a pout. "I want
sparkling water."

"I'm sorry," Tim said.

"That's the best they can do here," Sarah explained.
"At least with the bottled water you won't get sick. That's
why we can't drink from the tap here, because the water
might be contaminated."

"Contaminated?"

"There are lots of parasites in the drinking water.
Even water taken from a spring, which is where we get it
here. You're not even supposed to brush your teeth with
the tap water."

Ack! I had already rinsed out my mouth with the tap
water. "What if you only did it once?"

"It's probably okay," Sarah said. "Just don't do it again."

"Yeah, you'll be fine, I'm sure," Tim said. "They just
want you to be really careful, that's all. Here, feel my hand,"

he said as he laid it down on the table in front of Sarah and me.

Wow, that was random. What in the world did that have to do with the drinking water?

"Gosh, I can't believe how rough it is," Sarah said, as she ran her hand along his.

Yeah, except I was pretty sure she wasn't the one he was aiming for with that little invitation.

"Check it out," Tim said to me.

Yes, right again!

I quickly ran my fingers over his palm. It was like sandpaper.

"I even got a couple of calluses."

Charming.

"I bet you won't forget your work gloves again," Sarah said.

"Not likely, but I wasn't going to miss out on all the fun of building the school!"

Physical work and *fun* were two concepts that I didn't normally put together in the same sentence, unless there was irony, dark humour, or sarcasm involved.

"Did they run out of gloves?" I asked, hopeful that they wouldn't have a pair for me and I could avoid working.

"We're supposed to bring our own gloves," Sarah said. "You did bring gloves, didn't you?"

I shook my head.

"But it was right there in the information package."

There had been some preachy, long-winded email they'd sent that was an automatic delete. "I really didn't have time," I tried to explain. "I didn't even know I was coming until about a week ago."

"But how did you have enough time to raise the funds for the trip?" one of the girls, Andrea, asked.

"I didn't raise funds. My father just wrote a cheque."

"Your father must be rich!" Sarah exclaimed.

Well, duh!

"Not rich. Just comfortable." I wasn't supposed to brag about how much money we had, but compared to almost everybody else that I knew, yeah, we were rich.

"My father says that Donald Trump is rich," I mentioned.

"Yeah, he is rich, for sure," Tim agreed.

Now was the time for the bragging part. "And he's truly a very nice man."

They all stopped eating, mid-chew, and looked at me with a curious blend of surprise, doubt, awe, and confusion.

"You know Donald Trump?"

"I wouldn't say I know him well. I've only met him a few times. And I've been over to his home, well, at least *one* of his homes, the spacious penthouse he owns on the Upper East Side of Manhattan . . . very nice. Either he has great taste or a great designer."

"But how, *why*, do you know him?" Tim asked.

"My father has done some business deals with him."

"That is so cool! Hey, did he ever say to your father, 'You're fired!'?"

"You obviously don't know my father." I chuckled. "He didn't work *for* The Donald, they were more like partners." My father being the very junior partner, but these guys didn't need to know that.

I could tell by everybody's expressions that they were seriously impressed. A little name-dropping goes a long way, as long as you drop the right name. I made a mental note to strategically drop a few more along the way in the coming weeks. Realistically, this group was so out of the mainstream that I could claim to know just about anybody and they wouldn't even have a clue if I was making it up. The secret to telling a lie is to keep it simple enough to remember, but to add just enough odd details to make it credible.

"I don't know what I can do now," I said. "I didn't bring gloves, and it isn't like I can buy them out here."

"You could use mine," Tim offered.

This was where I wanted him *not* to help.

"That's sweet, but you need yours. If those calluses get worse you might not be able to work at all, and I wouldn't want to be responsible for that."

"It's all right," Sarah said. "Renée told me she has some extra pairs."

"Then why didn't she offer Tim a pair?"

"She has them here at the centre, not at the school. Be sure to mention it to her and she'll bring along a pair for you," Sarah said.

"I'll do that," I said. That is: *I'll do that when hell freezes over or I wear something off the rack from Wal-Mart, whichever comes first.* By not mentioning it to Renée I could get away with not working for at least one day, or at least not working at anything that was too physical. Maybe I could supervise.

"It would be a shame to get those hands all roughed up," Tim said. "They look so soft."

I smiled. With the price I paid for moisturizer and hand creams they'd better be soft.

"I just can't get over your nails," Sarah said as she picked up one of my hands and looked more closely.

I didn't know if she'd notice that the colour was a perfect complement to my earrings. I turned my head slightly and brushed back my hair with the other hand to let her have a clear look. She just continued to stare at my nails.

Subtle wasn't something that was going to work well with this group—even *obvious* subtle.

"How do you get them so perfect?" Sarah asked.

"I have a little help," I said. "They're acrylic."

"You have fake nails!" Sarah exclaimed loudly.

I gestured for her to keep her voice down. "I wouldn't say 'fake,' really, Sarah, but they are artificial."

"I never would have guessed," she said.

"That's the idea. The secret is to keep your look natural—they should be long enough to look good and get noticed, but not too long. Nothing is worse than those people who wear their nails like claws. Claws are for witches and wild—"

My last words were cut off by a loud, irritating sound. We all stopped talking and turned toward it. The man who had offered me coffee was holding a large metal handbell, like the ones that teachers use to call kids in from recess.

"Supper is ready," he said. He gestured to a long counter set with platters and bowls of food, with plates and cutlery stacked up at one end.

People started to get to their feet.

"A buffet. How quaint. It must be like having your meal at an all-you-can-eat place."

"I *love* those places!" somebody said, and I had no doubt he wasn't offering any sarcasm there. He was obviously one of those people who equated quantity with quality.

"I can get you a plate if you like, and you can stay seated," Tim offered. "I know you're still probably pretty tired."

"That's sweet," I said, and he actually blushed and looked down at his feet. "But I can serve myself."

I got up. He'd have no idea what I'd like—if anything. And besides, I'd discovered early on in life that monopolizing the only decent-looking boy in a group was a really bad way to win friends and influence people. Who knew? I might end up needing some of these girls more than I needed him.

CHAPTER ELEVEN

"While everybody is finishing up their desserts," Renée called out, "we're going to start our seminar."

Seminar . . . that sounded suspiciously like school. I had signed up for diversion, not education. Well, they could make me come here and they could talk at me, but they couldn't make me listen . . . and they certainly couldn't make me learn.

"All of you—with the exception of Alexandria, who hasn't had the opportunity yet—have met and worked with the Maasai people. Tonight we're going to learn more about their culture, history, and traditions. Assisting me today will be Nebala."

He stepped out of the shadows. He was still in his red dress and blanket combination. I got the feeling his wardrobe was fairly limited and strictly in shades of red. Better than an orange jumpsuit, but not much.

He was also holding a spear. Talk about stereotyping yourself. Slung over his shoulder were a wooden bow and some kind of canister that I assumed held arrows. Unless the bow was just to hit somebody over the head with.

"This is," Renée said, motioning to Nebala, "the most feared individual in all of Africa. He is a Maasai warrior."

I guess I could see how he might be scary—to Fred Flintstone. Just about anything from an AK-47 all the way down to a musket would have been more dangerous. He'd only scared me at the airport because he'd practically jumped out of the dark and tried to steal my luggage.

"According to Maasai legend, these people came from the north, in what is now the Sudan," Renée explained. "They are nomadic herders of cattle, and they followed their herds south looking for pasture. To the Maasai, their cattle are second in importance only to their family."

If I'd known I was in for this I would have brought along my iPod. I'd spent a lot of time in class perfecting how to intertwine the cord with my necklaces, put it behind my neck, and then have the earbuds hidden by my hair. I'd made it through grade ten math with a sixty-eight average with music in one ear and the *blah, blah, blah* of the teacher in the other. I know I could have gotten a higher mark with both ears open, but we all have sacrifices we need to make.

"Of all the tribal groups of Kenya, the Maasai have stayed closest to their traditional way of life. Because of this, they are often viewed by the other groups as the most backwards people, rejecting western ways . . ."

Except for maybe their cellphones.

" . . . while, on the other hand, they are respected by others because of their pride in their heritage. And pride is one of the most important characteristics of the Maasai people. This is intertwined with honour, integrity, and, of course, legendary bravery."

I guess you would have to be pretty brave to continually appear in public wearing a blanket.

"I mentioned cattle as being important to the Maasai, but I need to talk about them more. The Maasai describe themselves as, simply, keepers of cattle. A man's wealth is measured by the number of cattle he owns."

I almost laughed, and then thought better of it. After all, there was a certain logical sense to it. Cows were visible, countable, and out there for everybody to see. They were like Mercedes, mansions, and expensive clothes and jewellery, except easier to evaluate. There was also no need to try to figure if somebody had overextended themselves and the bank actually owned what they were using. I didn't think there was a credit system for cows. Either you owned them or you didn't. It wasn't like some bank somewhere was going to foreclose on your cattle.

"Maasai legend also says clearly that all the cattle in the world belong to them. So when other people have cattle, the Maasai believe that they are illegally in their possession, and a Maasai is simply reclaiming what is his when he takes the cattle back."

"Takes back?" a boy asked. "Do you mean they steal other people's cows?"

"The Maasai don't consider it stealing as much as reclaiming."

"Where I come from they call it rustling, and people take that mighty serious," he said.

There was a twang in his voice that made me believe that he probably did take cows very seriously. That was rather bizarre . . . and pathetic, and kind of sad.

"They take it very seriously here, too," Renée said. "There was a major clash between members of two groups just last week about fifty miles from here." She turned to Nebala. "Do you know what happened?"

"Eleven killed. Two Maasai."

I shook my head. Killed for a bunch of cows? But I sort of understood. Cows, money, jewellery, gold, oil— what was the difference?

"These conflicts are much, much less common than in the past," Renée emphasized. "But obviously they still exist. And in these conflicts, the Maasai believe that it is not murder to kill a member of another tribal group."

"They can just kill somebody and it's not murder?" that same boy questioned. Somehow stealing cows didn't seem quite as serious.

"No, the Kenyan government does not agree with Maasai beliefs. They will arrest anybody who commits assault, murder, or theft of cows," Renée said. "Now, going back, once again, to cattle. Traditionally a Maasai meal often involves both milk and blood from the cattle."

A whole bunch of people groaned.

"Blood . . . they drink blood?" I gasped. Were these people from Kenya or Transylvania?

"Yes, they make an incision on the neck," Renée said. "But it's rarely done these days. Mainly just for ceremonial purposes or a traditional gathering."

"In my house we just order an ice cream cake from Baskin-Robbins," Sarah said, and everybody laughed.

"Nebala?" Renée asked.

"I'd rather have a Tusker."

Renée and the other staff members burst into laughter. Everybody else looked at them like they were crazy.

"Tusker is the most popular brand of beer in Kenya," Renée explained. "And I, too, would prefer a cold Tusker to a warm mixture of blood and milk. Now, I'll turn things over to Nebala, who will tell us about how a Maasai boy becomes a man."

Nebala stepped into the middle as Renée retreated. He drew back his blanket to reveal his weapons. He took out that wooden club thingy and placed it on the table.

"This is the *konga*. It can be held as a club in close contact fighting or thrown at a target far away."

Next he drew a long knife from a sheath still hanging on the belt. It made a swishing sound as it was withdrawn.

"This is a sword," he said as he held it up. The light glistened off the edge as he slowly turned it. It looked razor-sharp. "The purpose of this is obvious." He placed it on the table beside the *konga*.

He then took the bow and the long canister off his shoulder. He opened the canister and pulled out an arrow. "For smaller targets at a distance. Sometimes the tip of the arrow is dipped in poison made from a plant root."

"I should note that Nebala, like all Maasai, is an expert on all the animals and plants of the Maasai Mara and how they can be used. In fact, he is an expert on all living things," Renée said.

"We also know about the stones, water, wind, stars, and sky. To us they are also living things with spirits."

He then picked up his spear. It was longer than he was tall. He held it up high and slowly turned it in his hand.

"This is the most important weapon," he said. His voice was now more quiet and solemn and serious as he looked at the spear. "It is with this spear that a boy must kill a lion." He looked up at us, and his expression was almost frightening. I had to work hard not to look away, even though he wasn't even looking directly at me.

"A group of young men go in search of a male lion. They surround the lion and then close in. The boy who strikes the lion first with his spear will receive the head, the mane. The one who strikes second is given the tail."

"No offence," one of the boys said, "but I'd want more than a spear if I was going to try to kill a lion."

"That does sound awfully dangerous," another added.

Nebala nodded in agreement. "Many die, almost all are wounded." He pulled aside his tunic and revealed a series of large scars on his arm and shoulder. "The lion struck me as I struck it."

There was a chorus of groans and giggles and comments.

"Did you kill it?" the first boy asked.

"If I hadn't, I wouldn't be here to tell of it. The spear went through its chest. It was my second kill."

"How many lions have you killed?" Christina asked.

"Seven."

"That seems so cruel, like such a waste," she said.

"To become a warrior, a boy must do this."

"It still seems cruel."

"Actually," Renée said, "the government wildlife services have just outlawed the practice. It is now illegal to kill a lion, except in self-defence or to eliminate an animal that has been consistently preying on a herd."

"That's good," Christina said.

"Is it?" I questioned, before I'd even thought not to speak.

Everybody looked at me.

"Well, I was just thinking, if killing lions is illegal now, how does a boy become a man?"

"Nebala?" Renée asked.

He didn't answer right away. He appeared to be staring off into the distance. Slowly he shook his head. "We don't know . . . we don't know."

"Does anybody else have any questions?" Renée asked.

Lots of people raised their hands. I had a question too, but I wasn't going to raise my hand like some little school-child. I'd just ask.

"You and the other Maasai I saw on the road always wear red. Why?" I asked.

"Some people believe it is a warning to the lion. He sees the red and runs away," Nebala explained. "Others say that the lion is attracted to the red because it looks like the blood of a fresh kill, so he goes for the warrior and leaves the cattle alone."

"Which is it?" I asked.

"Both."

"It can't be both," another person objected.

"One thing can be many things," he said.

I couldn't tell if that was really deep or if he was just quoting a bumper sticker or a fortune cookie.

"But most animals are colour blind," Christina said. "I'm pretty sure I remember reading somewhere that lions can't see colour. It's one of those myths, like bullfighters having a red cape because it attracts the bulls, even though they can't see colour either."

"I haven't read those books." Nebala smiled. "And neither have the lions. Maybe next time I am close to a lion I'll ask him his opinion."

There was a rush of giggles, including mine. Some people were laughing at his comment. Me, I was laughing at Christina for asking the question. She was *so* pretentious. So she had read things, big deal! We could all read.

"Other questions?" Renée said.

"If it's only murder when a Maasai kills another Maasai, how do they settle disputes between two warriors? Is there a court or judge or something?" one of the boys, Jimmy, asked.

Nebala picked up the *konga*.

"You hit each other?" Jimmy asked, sounding shocked.

"We throw the *konga* to see which man can toss it the farthest," Nebala said.

"And the farthest toss wins?"

"The one who throws the farthest gets to go first. Come, let me show you," he said to Jimmy.

Jimmy got to his feet, stumbled over his chair, and walked to the front. He looked nervous.

"Stand facing me, a few steps back," Nebala ordered Jimmy. "If I throw the farthest, then I get first throw . . . at you." He swung the club like he was going to throw it, and Jimmy screamed and jumped backwards. Nebala was still holding the *konga*.

"If the person flinches or moves, like that, then he loses the dispute."

"How about if he doesn't flinch?" somebody asked.

"If he survives the blow, then it is his turn to throw. They take turns until somebody moves or dies."

"How about if he doesn't flinch, but it hits him in the head and kills him?" a third boy asked.

"Then he dies with great honour," Nebala said.

Without thinking I laughed, and everybody turned to me.

"Alexandria?" Renée asked. "Something about this strikes you as funny?"

"Not really . . . it's nothing."

"There must be something," Christina said, "or you wouldn't have laughed. Please share with us. There's no need to be afraid to talk."

I knew what she was doing. Neither of us was holding a *konga* but this was a challenge. I wasn't going to be the one to flinch.

"I was thinking that the Maasai remind me of the Klingons on *Star Trek*."

Christina broke into laughter, like I had said the stupidest thing in the entire world. A few others joined in, but not with the same enthusiasm. I remained straight-faced, not moving, not showing emotion.

"You can't seriously compare some bad television show with the proud culture of the Maasai peop—"

"I always thought the same thing," Nebala said, cutting her off.

"You know *Star Trek?*" Christina gasped.

"I went to college in Nairobi. I live in Kenya, not on Jupiter."

This time everybody laughed—everybody except Christina.

"On that note, I think we should all settle in for the night. Morning will come early . . . *very* early," Renée said, looking directly at me.

People got up and started off to bed without complaint or discussion. These weren't teenagers, they were like really, really well-behaved six-year-olds. Very wimpy six-year-olds.

As everybody filed out of the dining room and set off for their tents, I moved over to Nebala. He was putting his weapons on again.

"Did you really always think that Klingons are like the Maasai?" I asked, so quietly that nobody else could hear.

"That's what I said."

"That wasn't the question."

He didn't answer. I wasn't going away until he did.

"Well?"

"I did watch the show sometimes, and I can see your point."

"But you never thought about it before, right?"

He shook his head.

"Then why did you say it? Why did you agree with me?" I asked.

He smiled. "You didn't flinch."

CHAPTER TWELVE

"That wasn't pleasant," Sarah said. Her hair was wet and she was trembling.

"The water was incredibly cold," Andy agreed. Lucky for her, though, she didn't have enough hair to really worry about a decent shampoo.

"Freezing," I agreed. "I was the first one in line to shower this morning and it was cold for me, too. There must be something wrong with the heater."

What was wrong with the heater was that it wasn't big enough to supply hot water beyond the first thirty minutes of my shower. Ha! So much for not being able to take a long, hot shower. I would have loved to have pointed that out to Renée, but I figured that wasn't such a great idea. I'd just keep my mouth shut and smile. She was wrong and I was right!

"Your hair still looks good," Sarah said.

"Cold water works the same as hot . . . not that *I'm* complaining about the cold. After all, so many people in

Africa have no water at all, so who are we to complain that ours isn't hot enough?"

That shut everybody up pretty quickly. This was hardly a challenge. These people were all so dedicated and earnest and guilt-ridden that I could play them like a piano.

"Aren't you going to wear a bandana around your hair?" Sarah asked.

"I don't think so." Certainly not in this life.

"Aren't you worried about the road dust and the concrete dust?" Andy asked.

"Not really." They could roll up the windows for the drive, and I wasn't getting anywhere near concrete or its dust. Unfortunately, I had *forgotten* to mention to Renée my need for work gloves, and surely it had to violate at least some safety law for me to work without them.

"And your clothes are so beautiful, aren't you afraid of ruining them?" Sarah asked. "They look so expensive."

She was actually kind of sweet to be worried about that. I was wearing a darling little Lilly Pulitzer flower-print tunic and matching capris from the resort wear line.

"Honestly, these are the least expensive clothes I have," I told her—and really, it was true. But okay, maybe the Prada sneakers were worth worrying a bit about. Never mind, I wasn't planning on doing enough work to ruin anything, except Renée's plan to force me to do hard labour.

"Let's get to the truck," somebody called out, and I followed the rest of the gang in a little line. This was not good. Being in the back of the line meant a greater chance of being in the back of the truck. Regardless, maybe I could convince whoever was in the truck to let me take their place. I knew if it was Tim or one of the other boys I could probably convince him to run along beside the truck. But I did have a backup plan.

All that dust couldn't be good for my asthma. It might even trigger an attack, a *severe* asthma attack. At least, it might if I actually had asthma, but who would know that? I could hyperventilate with the best of them. When I was little I'd sometimes hold my breath until my parents gave me what I wanted. That might still work.

Everybody seemed happy and pumped. Lots of chatter, laughter, playful teasing, and smiles. These were happy, happy, *happy* people. They were like the Stepford children. Did they think we were going shopping?

Sarah followed the little line leading up the ladder and into the back of the truck. This was where we were going to part company.

"I'm going to ride up front," I said.

She looked down from the ladder. She looked sad. "You'll miss all the fun."

"What sort of fun?" I asked, although I was pretty sure it wasn't going to be anything I would really regret missing.

"We sing songs and play games!" she exclaimed.

"I don't know, Sarah, a person can only take so much of a good thing. Save me a little chunk of that for tonight."

I went to the front and started to climb in when I remembered that the passenger seat was on the other side. I had no interest in driving this thing. I had my heart set on my Mercedes, not some broken-down old truck. I circled around the front and practically bumped into Renée.

"I thought I'd keep the driver company," I said.

"I'm afraid he's going to have to survive without your sparkling wit. Everybody rides in the back."

"I would but . . . don't you think it would be better for somebody with asthma to ride up front, so the dust doesn't trigger an attack?" I asked.

"It would be, if somebody had asthma."

"*I* have asthma."

"No you don't," she said.

"Don't you think that I might know if I had asthma or not?" I demanded.

"I agree, you'd really think you would know, but apparently you don't. You are allergic to penicillin, and develop a skin rash when exposed to certain man-made fibres."

"Like polyester," I said.

"I'm surprised polyester ever got close enough to your skin for you to know that." She chuckled.

If that was an attempt at an insult, she'd missed by a mile.

"But you don't have asthma, and I have the medical records to prove it."

I remembered my mother having to fill out forms, but I didn't know what they were for. Now I knew.

"It's just recent. I just developed it."

"Really? So where's your puffer?"

I opened my mouth to say something and then realized it was pointless. There was no reason to wage a war you couldn't win, and this one was over. I turned on my heel and started to walk away.

"Hold on!" she called out, and I stopped. *Here it comes, the big lecture about lying.*

"You can't wear that necklace."

My hand went up to touch it. I hadn't even thought about it. I knew there were places where you shouldn't go wearing expensive jewellery, and this was certainly worth a lot of money.

"Where can I put it?" I asked.

"I'll lock it in the glove compartment of the truck."

I was going to take it off and hand it to her, but first I had a question.

"Will it be safe there?"

"As safe as it would be around your neck," she answered.

"But aren't we putting it away because it's *not* safe for me to wear?"

"Theft is no danger whatsoever. Weren't you listening to anything that we talked about last night?"

I resented that comment. To my surprise, I'd listened to everything.

"These people are Maasai. They think they own all the cattle in the world, not all the gold and diamonds. They would never take your necklace. Matter of fact, if you accidentally dropped it a Maasai would walk for days to return it to you. Integrity is as much a part of their culture as bravery."

"Then why can't I wear it?"

"It's disrespectful," she said.

"How can a necklace be disrespectful?" I'd been accused of having attitude myself many times, but never my jewellery!

"How much is that thing worth?" Renée asked.

"Isn't that a little personal? Besides, it was a present, so I really don't know."

"But you must have a rough idea. It's gold, right?"

"Of course."

"And those stones are diamonds, I'm sure. How many diamonds?"

"Fifteen. It was my fifteenth-birthday present from my grandmother."

"So it would be safe to say that the necklace is worth at least a couple of thousand dollars."

"It would be safe to say that it's worth more than twice that amount," I said.

"Okay, say four thousand dollars. Each dollar is worth

sixty-four Kenyan shillings, so your necklace is worth around twenty thousand shillings."

"Twenty-five thousand and six hundred," I said.

She looked puzzled.

"Four thousand multiplied by sixty-four. I can do simple math in my head."

"Okay, if you say so, twenty-five thousand and six hundred shillings. The people at the school we're visiting today live on less than fifty shillings a day."

"That can't be right, that's only about seventy-eight cents."

"You did that in your head too?" she asked.

"Yes, although I rounded it down. It was seventy-eight point one five, but you said it was *less* than fifty shillings so I thought it was okay. Regardless, nobody can live on that amount of money. It isn't right."

"It isn't right. It's horribly wrong. But it is a fact. Somehow they survive on that amount of money. So, the daily existence of how many people is hanging around your neck?"

Fifty-one thousand, two hundred was the answer. I didn't give it. I handed her the necklace and walked away.

Everybody but Nebala was already in the back of the truck. He stood at the bottom of the ladder.

"It is a good day to die," Nebala said to me.

"What?"

"It is a good day to die. Isn't that what Klingons say before they go into battle?"

Despite everything I burst out laughing. Everybody in the truck looked down at us for a second and then went back to talking. I held out my right hand, my four fingers split into a v shape.

"Live long and prosper."

He smiled from ear to ear. So what if he knew I was a closet Trekkie? It wasn't like he was going to tell anybody I knew, or that I was going to run into him at the mall or at a party.

I climbed up the ladder and into the back. I was greeted by a chorus of "Hello"s as if I'd been gone for a month. These people just didn't get *cool* at all. Reluctantly I waved back.

There were two rows of twinned seats and a big long bench seat along the back. Where should I sit?

"Come back here and we'll make room!" Sarah yelled out. Once again, Sarah to the rescue.

There was an open seat beside my dear roommate. I squeezed past her. Much better to be wanted and popular, especially with her looking on. Nobody had made space for *her* or even taken the available space beside her. They probably didn't want to hear a lecture about something she'd read, heard, or thought.

I shuffled sideways down the aisle toward the little gap they had made on the bench seat.

Sarah was on one side of the opening and Mary Beth on the other. I'd never met anybody with two first names before, although it seemed like something half the beauty pageant winners in the world had in common. She smiled at me. Poor dear. With her looks she'd need two plastic surgeons instead of two names if she ever wanted to win Miss America. She was sweet, though, so she would have got my vote for Miss Congeniality. I flopped down in the little seat and they both gave me a hug. Definitely Miss Congeniality.

The truck rumbled and then roared and then took off. This wouldn't be so awful—it was only a few miles. I'd endured this truck for six hours, so ten minutes wasn't going to be any great problem. Then the truck hit a gigantic bump and everybody was thrown into the air. I'd somehow conveniently forgotten just how bad these roads could be. A few miles wouldn't be just a few minutes.

"How about if we sing a song?" somebody called out, and before I could even think to yell, "No, let's not!" a chorus of people screamed out agreement.

"I know which one," Sarah said.

"Me too!" Mary Beth agreed.

"*Jambo, jambo bwana!*" Sarah sang.

"*Habari gani!*" she and Mary Beth sang together.

And then everybody else joined in. I didn't know the song. I didn't know the words. And even if I had known the words I still wouldn't have known what they meant— no wait, *jambo* meant hello, didn't it? I just knew this ride had suddenly gotten longer.

The truck ground to a stop and I lifted my head from my hands. Everybody got up and started toward the ladder to climb down.

Sarah knelt down in front of me. "Are you feeling better?"

"A little." How embarrassing. I'd almost lost my breakfast on this trip. I'd never been carsick before in my life, but this wasn't a car, and this wasn't a road, either.

"It is pretty rough back here," Sarah offered.

"How could a few miles take so long?" I groaned.

"It was just under an hour. Come on, you'll feel better when you get your feet on the ground."

She took me by the hand and led me down the now

empty aisle. Everybody else had already gotten off. She climbed down the ladder and I followed. Nebala offered me his hand for the last two steps and I accepted. He flashed me the Vulcan greeting and walked off.

"What was that?" Sarah asked.

"Must be some Maasai thing," I offered.

We rounded the truck and joined the group. They were clustered around Renée and a couple of guys who looked like workmen. I looked past them, trying to survey the whole scene. There were a dozen little buildings arranged around the property. A couple of the buildings were made of concrete blocks, topped with identical red tin roofs, with blue window frames and doors. They were cute in a dollhouse sort of way. The rest of the buildings weren't quite so cute. The roofs were rusty and they seemed to be constructed of mud.

In the distance was a large field with a couple of semi-matching soccer nets made of tree branches at each end, and off to the side were two rusty poles with basketball hoops attached. The whole area was a combination of burnt brown grass and red dirt. It certainly had less in common with the playing fields at my school than it did with the moon.

I heard children's voices and looked around. I could hear them but I couldn't see them. They had to be inside the buildings. Then I saw a face. A little tiny black face was peeking out of one of the windows. It was joined by a second and then a third face, and then a little hand waved at me. I waved back, and the little faces burst into laughter and disappeared from view.

"Okay, everybody, you all know what to do!" Renée announced. "Let's get to work!"

The group scattered. Apparently they all knew their

jobs. I would have paid more attention, but I already knew mine—my job was to avoid doing *any* job.

"Um . . . Renée," I called out. "I noticed that everybody is putting on their gloves, and I realized that I didn't bring any gloves. I was wondering if—"

She whipped a pair of gloves out of her back pocket and handed them to me. Without saying a word she walked away.

CHAPTER THIRTEEN

Wearing work gloves and actually working turned out to be not entirely the same thing. So far I'd managed to avoid all physical labour. In some ways, it had been almost as hard as the labour itself, but at least I wasn't going to end up all sweaty. I tried my best to avoid Renée, and that helped, but, as in fashion, the key to everything was in the accessories. I always had a shovel or a trowel in my hands. And when I walked, I walked with purpose. Maybe the only purpose was to get away from one place where there was work to another with less work, but if you were moving quickly people naturally figured you had some place to go and something to do when you got there.

My lack of effort didn't seem to be hindering the building process. The rest of the people were practically knocking themselves out. I almost got the feeling there was an unannounced contest between the church kids and the non-church kids to see who could do the most. I was content to be the referee. As far as I was concerned, the person who won this particular contest was the one who did the least work, and I was in first place with nobody else even in sight in my rear-view mirror.

"Alexandria, can I talk to you?" Renée asked.

"I'm sort of busy," I said. To illustrate the point I dug my trusty shovel into the pile of sand and actually put a shovelful into the wheelbarrow. So much for my shutout.

"I think we should talk, now."

Time for the backup plan. "Could I go to the bathroom first? . . . I really have to go . . . badly . . . Can you tell me where it is?"

She looked as if she wasn't going to tell me. Then, "Over there, the little building by the fence."

I looked in the direction she was pointing. That couldn't be a bathroom. It was just some little shack-like building . . . oh, no.

"It's an outhouse, isn't it?"

She nodded. "Ever used an outhouse before?"

"Once, at a cottage."

"So you've never used the bathrooms here at the school before, right?"

I shook my head.

"Then our conversation can definitely wait. Come, let me escort you."

"I think I can go to the bathroom by myself. I've been toilet-trained for a long time."

"I'm sure you have, but I'll walk you over there anyway. I doubt if you've been trained with these toilets."

I didn't know what *that* was supposed to mean, but she seemed pretty amused by it. What was so funny about me going to the bathroom?

"We'll talk when you're through," she told me.

I walked off toward the bathroom and didn't turn around, but I could hear her footsteps not far behind. I really didn't like this escort, mainly because the whole idea behind going to the bathroom was to distract her so we wouldn't have a conversation. Now she'd be right outside, waiting for me for me to come out. That wouldn't work . . . unless I just didn't come out. I could just sit there and wait, tell her I wasn't feeling well, and sit in there for an hour, or even more. It was out of the sun and I would be sitting down, and there definitely wouldn't be any heavy lifting or mixing of cement. Maybe that was a good Plan B. Besides, come to think of it, I really did need to go.

There were two little outhouses. Two was good—I could sit in one and there'd still be another one for everybody else.

I opened up the door and the smell hit me like a transport truck. I turned slightly away. There was no way I was going to sit in there for any longer than I absolutely had to. I took a breath of fresh air into my lungs and went to step in . . . there was no toilet. There was just a slab of concrete on the floor and a hole in the ground in the middle of it where the toilet should have been. This had to be the boys' toilet . . . like, a urinal thing.

I let the door close. Renée stood there smirking. I ignored her and pulled open the other door. It was exactly the same. Concrete, hole in the ground, no toilet.

I turned to Renée. "Where's the girls' bathroom?"

"You're holding the door to it."

"But . . . but there's no toilet."

"That hole in the middle is the only toilet you get."

Of all the bizarre things I'd seen, heard about, or been told, this was the most bizarre. This wasn't real. I looked at Renée closely. She looked pretty amused so did that mean she was just joking around?

"I really need to go," I pleaded. "Really, where are the toilets?"

"Really, right there."

"But there's no seat . . . how do I sit down?"

"You don't sit. You squat over the hole and go."

I looked at her, and then at the hole in the ground, and then back at her. This was not believable, this was not doable! I let the door slam shut with a loud thud and backed away, as if the toilet were a hand grenade. Renée had that trademark smirk on her face. She looked as though she was really enjoying my suffering.

"I thought you wanted to use the washroom," she said.

"I can't do that . . . it's not possible."

"It is possible. People across most of the world do it every day."

"It's not possible for *me* to do. I'm not squatting like some sort of animal."

"Are you calling these people animals?" Renée questioned.

"Of course not! It's just that . . . I can't do that, I won't do that."

"But I thought you had to go . . . *really* bad," she said.

"I did . . . I do . . . but I'm not going to use that hole. I'm just going to wait."

"We won't be back at the centre for at least four hours."

"I can wait four days if I have to. But this isn't what you wanted to talk to me about, is it?" Forget about going to the toilet distracting her from whatever she wanted to talk about. Now I wanted it the other way around.

"Nothing serious. I just wanted to see how you were doing."

That wasn't what I'd been expecting her to say. I'd thought she was going to come down on me for not working, and instead she seemed to be concerned about my welfare.

"I'm doing okay, I guess."

"You're probably wise to take it easy today," she said. "I've noticed you're playing it smart and not overexerting yourself."

Was this her way of telling me, without telling me, that she'd noticed I wasn't working very hard? Well, I wasn't playing that game. If she wanted to tell me off, then she could just go ahead and do it.

"As you get more settled in, get to know the work that has to be done, get your sleep cycles all in sync, then we'll expect you to work harder and harder. Not as hard as Sarah and her crew, but still a lot harder than you have today."

She was giving me a subtle lecture about not working. Subtle wasn't what I'd expected from her, but this was good. Subtle I could ignore.

"I think it's important for you to meet the people you're helping," Renée said. "I'm going to introduce you to the children."

"But aren't they all in class?" I asked, motioning to the empty schoolyard.

"They are, and that's where you're going to meet them."

Renée led. I followed. Familiar pattern. We stopped in front of a building. It was nothing like the one we were constructing. This one was made of wooden sticks and mud and . . . what was that sticking through the mud by the door?

"Watch out for the barbed wire," Renée said.

That's what it was! But why would there be barbed wire there? That made no sense.

"To construct the older school buildings they drove wooden poles into the ground and then wrapped barbed

wire around them to make a base," Renée said, answering
my unasked question. "Then they packed mud and cow
dung around the wire."

"Cow dung . . . you mean, cow poop?"

"Yes, it's sort of the mortar in the mix."

I shuddered. This building was being held together by
cow crap. That was beyond disgusting.

Renée knocked on the open door and we walked
through. I stopped, in shock, two steps in. This little room,
hardly bigger than my bedroom, was filled, wall to wall,
with kids. There had to be fifty or sixty of them, all packed
together, three or even four together on little wooden
benches behind even littler wooden desks. They looked to
be about ten or eleven years old. Each was wearing an
identical red woollen sweater over a white shirt or blouse
and a jumper-style dress for the girls, long shorts for the
boys. All of the kids, boys and girls, had close-cropped hair,
almost shaved right down. They were all, without exception, smiling and staring right at me. Nervously, I smiled
back, trying to hide how uncomfortable I felt.

The teacher came over and greeted Renée and then
shook hands with me as well. I felt awkward. They
exchanged words in that language—I'd learned it was
called Swahili.

I continued to look around. The floor of the room was
hard-baked red earth. The two little windows held broken
panes and wire mesh, and let little air or light into the stale,
dim room. There was an open textbook on each desk—
one book for everybody at the desk to share—and each
student was holding a little stub of a pencil overtop a small
exercise book. Up above were thin wooden beams holding
a rusting tin roof in place. I could see holes in the roof,
places where rain would get through. I was also surprised

by what wasn't there—there were no computers, no pictures or alphabets or decorations on the walls, no lights, no electrical outlets, no displays, no books, no nothing. It was a big, dark room with a dirt floor and walls made out of mud and cow crap, empty except for the kids who were practically piled on top of each other. And each kid, without exception, was smiling. What did they have to smile about?

Renée turned to the class and said hello to them all. "*Hamjambo!*"

"*Jambo!*" they all called out in response.

She turned to me. "Say who you are and say hello."

"Um, hello . . . *jambo* . . . *hamjambo,*" I said. I was pretty sure you said "*hamjambo*" when there was more than one person. I was feeling very self-conscious. "My name is Alexandria and I'm fifteen."

"Hello!" they yelled back. A bunch of them tried to say my name but it came out garbled.

"Your name is very long," the teacher explained.

"They could call me Alex," I suggested. I turned back to them. "I am Alex!" I said, touching my chest.

"Hello, Alex!" a boy called out, and the rest burst into laughter.

"This is Standard Six," Renée said. "Grade six. They're studying math."

I looked at the blackboard. There were long-division problems stretched from one side to the other. I remembered doing them . . . in about that same grade.

"Do you have any questions?" Renée asked.

I shook my head. "Not really . . . but there are a lot of students."

"There are seventy-four students enrolled in Standard Six. Today there are sixty-three in attendance."

"Thank you for your time," Renée said, and they shook hands.

As we started to leave I looked back over my shoulder and waved. They were all smiling and waving back.

"Goodbye, Alex!" a voice called out, and everybody else laughed.

"In the last few years the government has decided that school will be free for all children from Standard One to Standard Eight," Renée told me.

"So these kids don't pay to come to school?" I said.

"Well, they do have to pay for uniforms, books, and other supplies."

"That can't be much . . . is it?"

"For some, it's more than they can afford and they can't come to school. For others, they can't afford the time to be in school because there are things that need to be done for the family."

"Is that why so many kids were away today?" I asked.

"Some would be sick. There are lots of infections and illnesses caused by drinking unclean water."

"They shouldn't drink water that isn't clean."

Renée gave me an angry look. "Do you think they have a choice?" she asked. "There are no drinking fountains or even running water here. These kids—and it's usually the children—have to walk up to four miles to get water and carry it home on their backs or balanced on their heads."

"I didn't know," I sputtered.

Her expression softened. "I'm sorry. Of course you didn't know. It just gets me so angry, but I shouldn't be angry with you. Instead of coming to school they're either home sick because of the illnesses caused by the bad water or they're out carrying water instead. Some kids only come to school every second day because on the alternating days they're carrying water or finding firewood or tending to the flock or doing one of the thousand of things their families need them to do to survive."

"But there has to be something that can be done."

"We're talking about a fresh water project for this community. We want to either drill a well or create a rain-retention program that would capture water in the rainy season and store it in holding tanks."

"That would be good," I offered.

"It would, but either method costs money, and we're not exactly rolling in it."

"How much money?"

"A lot." She paused. "About the cost of your necklace."

The words jabbed at me like a punch to the stomach.

"Not that anybody's after your necklace. We're all doing our best. See how much better the new school building is going to be?"

"For sure. Concrete floors, solid stone walls held together with cement, windows with glass, and there's going to be more light and air."

"A big step up," Renée said. "Come on, let's go to the next class."

We'd moved from class to class. Some were a little bit better than the first but others were worse. The classes ranged from fifty-four students in Standard Seven to eighty-eight in Standard Two. All students shared the same red uniforms and the same smiles. Each student called out "*Jambo*" or

"Hello" and gave me a big smile or a laugh. In one class all the students got up and sang me a song—a beautiful song.

"This is our last stop," Renée said. "Standard Eight. Some of these kids will be your age or older."

I stopped at the door. "But if this is grade eight, how can they be my age? I'm going into grade eleven."

"Some of these students couldn't come when they were younger because of family responsibilities or lack of funds. They could even be a couple of years older than you."

She knocked and we entered. Before we'd even greeted the teacher I could see a big difference between this and the other classes. There weren't that many students. I did a quick count—nineteen—and each student sat at his or her own desk. On each desk was a large exercise book, and they hardly looked up as they continued to work.

"They are writing an examination," their teacher said, his voice just above a whisper.

"These are the tests they write to determine if they can go on to high school," Renée explained.

"Very difficult, very important," the teacher added.

I nodded. "So if they pass they can go on?"

"If they pass they're qualified to go on," Renée said. "They still need to be able to pay for classes. High school is not paid for by the government. The students and their families are responsible."

"And if they don't have the money?" I asked.

"Then this is the end of their schooling," Renée said. "That's why this class is so small. These are the only students who *might* have the ability *and* the money to go further. Even these tests they're taking have to be paid for by their families."

Renée turned to the teacher. "Thank you," she said, and we left the class.

I understood that people with money could afford more things, better things, than people who had no money, but didn't everybody have a right to education?

"That isn't fair," I said. "If you're smart enough you should be able to go to school."

"It isn't fair," Renée agreed, "but it isn't that much different from back home."

"It's way different!" I protested.

"Is it? What university are you planning on going to?" she asked.

"I don't know. Maybe Stanford, or UCLA. My mother wants me to go out east to Sarah Lawrence."

"All good schools."

"The *best* schools."

"And I guess anybody can just show up and get in, right?"

"Of course not. You have to have good marks, and do well on your SATs, and fill in applications, and—"

"And pay a lot of money," Renée said. "It doesn't seem fair that poor people can't go to university."

"But that's different. Everybody can go to high school, free."

"But lots of people drop out because they have to earn money to help their families survive, or they drop out because they know they can't go on further anyway and they know that with just a high school education you can't become a doctor or a lawyer or a teacher or a nurse," she said. "You can work at Wal-Mart with a grade-ten or a grade-twelve education, so why go further?" she asked. "Both countries place a roof on how far the poor can go. Here in Kenya, the roof is just lower."

I hadn't ever thought of that. There was so much that I'd never thought of, that I'd never needed to think about.

I suddenly felt my legs start to get all shaky and a rush of heat surged through my entire body.

"Are you okay?" Renée asked. She reached out and steadied me with one hand.

"I'm just feeling a bit woozy . . . nothing serious. I just feel like I need to sit down."

Renée took me by the arm and led me away from the school buildings and across the dusty schoolyard. I wasn't sure where we were going. Then I saw the big truck parked up ahead.

"Sit here, just rest against the truck."

I sat down and leaned against one of the big wheels on the shady side. It felt good to be sitting. Renée pulled out a bottle of water. She took off her bandana and poured water on it, then placed it around my neck.

"It's a hard adjustment," she said. "Not just the time changes and the travel, but dealing with the emotions. None of this is easy, is it?"

I shook my head.

"And I think in the end you might do okay," she said.

"But . . . but you don't think I am doing okay now . . . right?"

"Not yet . . . but I'm hoping. You just stay here, rest, and when you're ready, come back and join us."

I didn't answer. I just put my head down between my legs and closed my eyes.

CHAPTER FOURTEEN

I heard voices. Talking, whispering, giggling. I opened my eyes and almost screamed. All around me in a little semicircle were dozens and dozens of kids, staring and smiling and pointing at me as I sat on the ground. I shrieked and they roared with laughter, and some even jumped backwards.

"*Pateo!*" yelled out a loud voice.

A girl, an older girl, appeared in the gap between me and the children. She yelled something else and made a kicking gesture and the kids all screamed and scurried away. Whatever she'd said had scared them into leaving. She came and stood overtop of me.

"Okay?" she asked.

"I'm fine. I must have gone to sleep," I said.

She nodded. "A *cat* nap."

"Yes, I guess I had a catnap."

"May I?" she asked, gesturing to the space beside me.

"Sure. Sit down."

She sat down. "Ruth."

"No, I'm Alexandria."

She laughed. "*I* am Ruth."

"Oh, I didn't understand. Good to meet you."

"I am most pleased to meet you," she said.

She had a funny way of speaking, almost with a British accent, but her English was pretty good.

"Your hair is so long," she said.

"Not that long."

"To mine it is long," she said.

Her hair was, like that of almost all the girls, nearly shaved off.

"The colour . . . it is like straw."

"I think the exact term is honey-blond," I said, reciting the specific shade it was dyed.

"So beautiful."

"You should see how it usually looks," I said.

"Can I . . . touch?"

I was thrown for just a second. "Sure."

She reached over and very gently took a strand of my hair in her hand. "So soft . . . I wish my hair was like that."

So did more than half the girls in my school. "Yours is nice too," I offered.

She shrugged.

"Your English is very good," I told her.

"So is yours," she said, and laughed.

"Much better than my Swahili. Why is your English so good?"

"We start English in Standard Four. I am in Standard Eight. What Standard are you?"

"I'm going into grade . . . Standard Eleven."

"That is so good! Next year I hope to go to high school . . . if I can."

"Your English is very good, so you must be good at school."

She smiled and nodded. "Good, but maybe one of my brothers will go instead. We shall see."

"Why can't you both go?" I asked, before I realized the answer—money. It cost money to go to high school. Now I really wanted to change the subject. "How old are you?"

"Fifteen."

"I'm fifteen too!" I was just about to ask her why she was only in grade eight when I remembered what Renée had told me about kids here starting school late, or having to miss a lot of classes.

Ruth reached over and gently touched a finger to my eyelid. "Your eyes are colourful."

"Do you mean the eye or the colour around the eyes?"

"Both. Both. Very pretty."

"You have beautiful eyes too," I said. "So dark. And your cheekbones are perfect!"

"Cheekbones?"

"These are your cheekbones," I said, touching them. "You have cheekbones like a high-fashion model. Actually . . . stand up."

I got to my feet and she got up too. She was thin and tall, almost as tall as me. She made me think of the high-fashion models who were from Africa, like Iman.

"You really *could* be a model," I said.

She laughed and turned her eyes to the ground. Maybe for all I knew she'd even blushed, but I couldn't tell.

"Good to see you up and on your feet!" It was Renée. "And I see you've made a friend."

"This is Ruth."

"I know Ruth and her whole family," Renée said. The two of them hugged. "Are you feeling better?" she asked me.

"Better, but not right. I'm almost afraid to think how my stomach is going to react to the ride back. Do I really have to ride in the truck?"

"The only other option is to walk."

"*Could* I walk?"

"It's pretty far. Almost seven miles."

"I can walk that far. That's not a problem for me, honest, I'm a good walker. Sometimes when I'm shopping with my mother we're on our feet for the whole day!"

She almost laughed, and then politely stopped herself. "It's not just the distance. I wouldn't want you to get lost. One of us would have to go with you, and we're all busy here supervising."

"I could walk her," Ruth offered.

Renée looked as though she was thinking. "Your village is about halfway to the compound. You wouldn't mind if she walked with you as far as your village?"

Ruth shook her head. "Would not mind."

Renée looked directly at me. "This is not how we usually do things, but I think walking with Ruth might be a good experience. And that way you'll only have to take the truck halfway back. But you have to promise you'll do exactly what Ruth tells you, and you'll wait at her home until we come by in the truck to get you."

"I'll do that, I promise."

"If you promise, that's good enough for me," Renée said. "You know what, Alexandria? I believe that you're a person of your word, and since you've given me your word I know you'll keep it."

I knew at least one judge who would have disagreed

with her—I wasn't even sure I agreed with her opinion myself—but I wasn't about to say that now.

School had been dismissed, and while some kids were hanging around, playing soccer or basketball, and others were watching the construction going on, most had started for the gate and were beginning to walk home.

Renée said something to Ruth in Swahili and the two of them hugged. She turned to me.

"We're just going to work for another thirty or forty minutes and then clean up. Hopefully we'll be leaving in the truck in less than an hour. We'll see you at Ruth's village after that. Be safe, and be smart." Then, to my total surprise, she reached out and hugged me as well.

Ruth took me by the hand and we started to walk. I thought she would let go, but she didn't. She kept hold of my hand as we hit the road and started to walk. Part of me thought it was strange to hold hands, but I noticed that the other kids were doing the same thing. Not just girls, but boys as well. They all held hands as they walked—sometimes pairs of them, sometimes whole chains of kids.

We were in the middle of a huge pack of kids, all in their red uniforms, moving along the dusty red road. The road, which had seemed so rough in the truck, was even rougher on foot. There were gigantic ruts, large rocks, and places where the roadway had been washed out completely, leaving behind a sandy gully, with the occasional trickle of brown water running across it.

A little hand reached up and grabbed my free hand. It was a girl, maybe eight or nine. She smiled up at me.

"My sister," Ruth said. "How many sisters do you have?"

"None."

"None! That is awful! Just brothers."

"No, I don't have brothers either. I'm an only child."

Ruth looked sad. "Your mother died?" she asked.

"No, my mother is alive."

"Your father died?"

"No, he's alive too."

Now she looked confused. She shook her head. "Why only one child?"

"I don't know, exactly. Lots of my friends are only children. Sometimes people have two. I know a family with four kids, but most aren't that large. How many brothers and sisters do you have?"

"Eleven."

"No, how many brothers and sisters in your family?" I asked. She obviously hadn't understood the question.

"Eleven. Seven sisters and four brothers. With me, we are twelve children altogether."

Now *I* was confused. I'd never met anybody who had that many brothers and sisters. They could have formed their own soccer team and still had a substitute on the bench.

There were times when I thought it would be nice to have a sister—somebody to share clothes and plot with against our parents—but I couldn't even imagine that many.

"Sister," she said, pointing to a little girl walking in front of us. She looked around. She called something out and two other little girls waved and smiled. "Both sisters." She pointed down the road. "Two brothers are right there."

There were lots of kids, lots of boys. "Which ones?"

She yelled something but nobody turned around. Ruth bent down, picked up a rock, and threw it, hitting a boy in the back! He jumped into the air, howling.

"Brother."

He scowled at her and yelled something. He didn't look or sound too happy. I didn't need to understand

Swahili to get the general idea. Ruth yelled out something else and a bunch of kids, including the ones she'd identified, raised their hands. There were five of them, six if you included Ruth.

"I am the oldest so sometimes I must stay home to care for them . . . especially if our mother is not well. I take care of everybody."

"What about your father? Shouldn't he take care of things?"

She laughed and then said something in Swahili, and everybody else laughed too.

"What did you say?" I asked.

"I tell them our father would do the laundry and cook us supper tonight."

"Is it that funny to think he might do those things?" I asked.

"Fathers don't do women's work."

Obviously women's liberation wasn't the biggest concept around here.

"Our father is a warrior. He has to tend to the herd," she told me.

"Your father . . . he's killed a lion?"

"Many. You will see the manes when you come to my house."

As we continued to walk, the crowd of kids became smaller as some of them left the road and took off along smaller trails. While the land was basically flat there were little bumps and rises, and in the distance there were taller hills, covered with trees and bushes. I didn't see any houses, and I could see a long way into the distance, so we still had a long way to go. In the foreground there were only a few scattered trees.

"Ruth, are there lions around here?" I asked.

She shook her head. "Not right here."

That was reassuring.

"Not within a mile . . . maybe farther."

That was not *quite* as reassuring.

"My father says that lions can smell a Maasai and they don't come near. You are safe when you are with us."

I didn't know about lions but there were a lot of cattle. Some were grazing close to the road, even wandering across it as we walked, while others were off in the distance. Some of the herds looked very large. Then I noticed different animals intermixed with the cattle. I thought they were just big goats until I saw the stripes. There were zebras in amongst the cows! Along with them were deer-like animals, some little ones with pointy horns, and other, bigger ones, with twisty antlers. And finally I saw something even bigger and taller—three of them—giraffes, reaching up with their long necks to pull the leaves from a tree! I stopped walking and stared at them.

"Giraffes!" I said to Ruth, pointing.

She nodded. "A few. They don't bother anybody."

"It's just that they're . . . giraffes. That's pretty amazing, don't you think?"

"I guess. You don't have giraffes in your country?"

"Only in the zoo. They're . . . kind of freaking me out."

She shrugged her shoulders, as if to say it was no big deal. Nobody else seemed to pay any attention to them either. I guess for them it was like me seeing a squirrel or a pigeon or a fancy car or a shopping mall. Zebras and antelopes and giraffes were just no big deal.

"What sorts of things do you and your friends do to chill?"

"Chill? Um . . . we sit in shade to try to stay cool."

"No, no, not doing things to *get* cool, things that *are* cool. Things you do to chill out, hang, stay loose, relax."

She shook her head and looked confused.

"I'll give you some examples. My friends and I go down to Rodeo Drive and we shop. Prada, Gucci, Fendi, all of the best stores."

She looked as though she had no idea what I was talking about, as though she'd never even *heard* of these stores.

"And then we go to Starbucks—they have the best! I usually have an iced frappuccino." Again, no response. "A coffee."

She nodded and smiled. "Yes, coffee."

"And we go cruising, listen to tunes . . . if we've got a convertible we might take the top down and catch some rays."

"No top?" she asked.

"Yes, we drive in a car without a top."

"That is too bad. Maybe they can make a top for the car."

"No, no, you don't understand, there is a top but it's down so we can get the sun and be *seen*."

"Couldn't you be seen through the windows . . . doesn't it have windows?"

"Yes, it has windows and a top and . . ." This wasn't working. "And then we go to somebody's place and maybe watch MTV or listen to the latest tunes that we've downloaded from . . . you have no idea what I'm talking about, do you?"

She shook her head. "But it sounds very nice."

"And on weekends we get all dolled up and get together and some of us have fake IDs and we go clubbing."

"Clubbing . . . you mean like a *konga* . . . like you hit things?" she questioned.

"No, not a club, a *club*."

She didn't look any less confused. I really wasn't being very helpful. And then it hit me. There was absolutely nothing I could say that would impress her. She didn't know about the styles, makeup, cars, people, or places that defined my world. For a split second I was disappointed. Then I just felt relieved. Not only *couldn't* I impress her with any of this, I didn't *need* to impress her. It wasn't like I was afraid she'd pull out a new Gucci bag or flash a Cartier watch. She was just going to smile and hold my hand and walk along the road with me. It was almost free-ing. Sort of Zen-like.

"What sorts of things do you do after school?" I asked.

"Gathering wood. Getting water. Cooking."

"I meant for fun. What do you do for fun?"

She shook her head and shrugged her shoulders.

"With the other girls."

"We go together to get water."

"And that's fun?"

"We talk when we walk. Sometimes we sing or play games."

"How far do you have to go?" I asked.

"Not far. We walk about twenty minutes there. Twenty-five back."

"How come it takes longer to get back?"

"The water is heavy."

"But you have to do *some* things that are fun. Don't you play?"

"When I was little I'd skip or sing songs. Sometimes we'd kick a ball. Now I cook. If I have time before dark I study. I need to study for my exams."

I tried to think what my evenings were like. I'd watch TV, maybe listen to some music on my iPod, talk on the phone, go out shopping or dancing, hang out with my friends. No cooking and no cleaning—Carmella took care of all that. No gathering wood or water. I just turned on the tap or dove in the pool.

We'd been walking now for at least forty minutes. The road was basically flat but in those few sections where it went uphill, even slightly, I could feel the strain in my lungs. Where I lived was right at sea level. Here, we were thousands and thousands of feet up. No wonder all those marathon winners were from Kenya. They got used to the thin air, and when they ran something like the Boston or New York Marathon it would be like their lungs were just drinking in all that thick oxygen.

"Here," Ruth said, and she led me off the road, along with her brother and sisters and a bunch of other kids who were already headed in the same direction.

"Do all of these kids live in your village?" I asked. There had to be twenty or thirty of them.

"Yes."

"And you know everybody in your village, right?" I asked.

She nodded. "Those who are not my brothers and sisters are all my cousins. Everybody in the village is my family."

"The entire village?"

Again she nodded. "If they were not family, they would not live there."

Although I hadn't seen it originally, I soon saw where we were headed. On the horizon was what looked like a large wooden fence. The closer we got, the more detail I could make out. It wasn't a fence, more like the wooden walls of an old-time fort. There were wooden stakes— really tree branches—driven into the ground, and between them were piles and piles of thorn bushes that formed a thorny wall.

"Is that your village?"

"Yes, we live there. All of us."

The thorn branches made it appear to be impenetrable. We started to circle around and I was impressed by just how big it was. It looked as though it wrapped around the whole village. There was a little gap, about the size of a driveway, and we walked through.

Inside, the fence was lined with small mud huts. It was like a gigantic circular townhouse development. And in the very middle was a large, muddy field. Why would they do that?

The kids scattered, running across the field, and were greeted by women, who seemed to be in front of all the little huts. Judging from all the chickens and goats wandering around and the way the field was beaten down and muddy, this had to be something like a corral for livestock, and all those little buildings were probably chicken coops or little mini-barns or workshops—sort of like garages when you don't have cars.

Ruth led me by the hand across the mud. I quickly realized that the mud was dotted with enormous piles of cow dung. These seemed to be everywhere. On the upside, that meant lots of new building material for the huts. I tried to envision just how many cows could be in a space this big. I had no idea, but I knew it had to be a whole lot.

Ruth stopped in front of a woman sitting on a little bench in front of one of the huts. She was very, very pregnant. She was working with a bowl filled with something. Food, I guessed . . . maybe cornmeal or something like that.

"This is my mother," Ruth said. She said something in

Swahili, and the only word that sounded out of place was my name.

Her mother looked up at me and smiled and nodded. Everybody smiled all the time. Everybody always seemed so friendly, so happy.

"Hello, I'm pleased to meet you," I said.

"My mother does not speak English."

"Oh, sorry. *Jambo.*"

Her smile got even bigger and she started talking to me, quickly, in Swahili. Ruth said something to her and she stopped and laughed.

"What did you say to her?" I asked.

"I told her that you don't speak Swahili. She thought you did."

"I just know a few words, a few phrases."

"You speak them well," Ruth said. "Like you are Maasai."

Now I laughed.

"I could teach you more Swahili," Ruth said. "You could teach me English."

"Your English is already excellent."

"I could practise with you, learn more about . . . *chilling.*"

"I can teach you the words, but I don't think the concepts apply."

Again she gave me a confused look.

"Will you show me your house?"

"Yes, yes, come." She took me by the hand and led me toward the little hut and she ducked down to go inside. I stopped. Obviously her English wasn't as good as I thought.

"No, your *house* . . . where you live."

"This is house. Come."

I ducked my head to get through the low doorway. Inside I could stand up, but just barely. The roof was scarcely higher than my head. It was dim in there and the air was smoky and thick. There was a small fire going, coals glowing below a metal grate. The only light that wasn't coming from the doorway was peeking in around the top, where the metal roof sat roughly upon the mud walls.

Ruth led me through another doorway, ducking to get underneath. "This is my room."

There was nothing but a large wooden box in the centre and rugs—no, skins—in piles on either side of the box. If this was her room, where did she sleep? There was no bed . . . no, she couldn't just sleep on the floor!

"Girls' side," she said, pointing to some skins. "Boys."

"You all sleep in here together, all twelve of you?"

She picked up a skin. It was striped, zebra. "Each has their own skin."

I didn't know what to say, how to react. I just knew that it felt as if the walls were closing in on me, that the air was getting thick. The air *was* thick. Thick and smoky, and I could taste it in the back of my mouth. I had to get out of there.

"Can we please go outside? . . . I'd better get out by the road to wait for my ride."

CHAPTER FIFTEEN

"Can I come in?"

I looked up. It was Renée, standing just outside the door of the tent.

"Could I stop you from coming in if I wanted to?" I asked.

"Of course you could, but you'd miss out. I brought you something."

That did perk my interest. "Well, in that case . . ."

She undid the zipper and stepped inside.

"Tents are tricky because there's no place to knock. Here."

She handed me a bottle of water and a plastic bag containing three pieces of bread.

"How appropriate. Bread and water for the prisoner."

"I noticed you didn't eat much at supper. I thought the bread might settle your stomach, and the water is to keep you hydrated. Are you still not feeling well?"

"I feel fine. I just wasn't that hungry."

She sat down on Christina's bed. Christina was hanging out with the church kids, who were probably learning some new inspirational songs or clapping games for the back of the truck. I imagined she'd prefer anything to butting heads with me again.

"I have a question," Renée said. "Tonight, when you were talking to the people serving, you were speaking to them in Swahili."

"Not really speaking, just saying 'please' and 'thank you' and a few other phrases."

"So you *knew* what you were saying."

"Don't look so shocked just because I picked up a few words."

"That's not the part that shocked me. It's that I've never heard you be polite in *English* before, much less a foreign language."

"Ha ha. Well, maybe I'm still waiting for you to do something that deserves thanks. Tell me, how thankful should a prisoner be to her keeper—no, that's the wrong term—her *warden?*"

"I'm not your keeper or your warden. This isn't prison."

"Club Med doesn't usually involve guards, electric fences, locked gates, and forced labour."

"I'm not sure if the work you did today could be called either 'forced' or 'labour,'" she said.

"I got that message."

"Alexandria, it's important that you know where you stand. What I'm going to put in the report for the judge."

"You're writing a report?" This was news to me.

"That's the way it works. How else would he know if you passed or failed the diversion program? You do know that you can fail, right?"

"Now that sounds like a threat. Am I supposed to thank you for threatening me?"

"Maybe you are. At least I'm going to hold you accountable and make you do what you're capable of doing instead of letting you flake out by playing the empty-headed, blond rich girl."

"If that was an attempt at a compliment you've missed by quite a margin."

"Not a compliment. A fact. There's more going on up there than you'd have people believe."

"You're telling me I'm not as stupid as I look? Thanks."

"No, I'm telling you that you're not as stupid as you *act*. For example, did you study Swahili before you came on this trip?"

"I didn't even know what Swahili *was* until I arrived here. I thought you were speaking African."

"Africa is a continent, not a country or a linguistic group."

"I know that," I snapped. Although I hadn't really known it until Sarah and Mary Beth had explained it to me.

"Regardless, already you've picked up a lot of basic Swahili. You really have a talent for language."

"That's what Carmella always says to me."

"Is she a friend?"

I huffed. "She's our maid, and she's Mexican."

"And you don't have any friends who are Mexican?" Renée asked.

"Well . . . there really aren't any Mexicans around my neighbourhood except for the maids, and of course the people tending to the gardens and lawns. It's not like there are any at my school."

Renée didn't look pleased with my answer. I knew her

type—left-wing liberals who thought we should all be friends. How could I be friends with people I didn't know and would never meet?

"So, if there are none of those people around, how did you learn to speak Spanish?" she asked.

"I *don't* speak Spanish, I speak *some* Spanish. Really, I understand it more than I speak it," I explained. "It's always good to know what people are saying about you."

"But how did that happen? How did you learn the language?"

"How should I know? Little snippets of conversation I heard, reading billboards that are bilingual, flipping through the channels and stopping on a Spanish soap opera for a few minutes . . . things like that."

"If you can understand it, then you can learn to speak it. Do you know what worlds that could open up for you?" she asked.

"It would mainly mean I could give orders to the gardener or order at a Tex-Mex restaurant. Aside from that, I don't think any."

"It would mean that you could speak to hundreds of millions of people around the world who speak Spanish!" she exclaimed. "You could travel through all of Central and South America!"

"Yes, I was planning on doing that next weekend," I said sarcastically. "Besides, I've heard that English is the most popular language in the world."

"Actually, Mandarin is spoken by the most people. English is the most common second language."

"Okay, whatever, even better. That means that people around the world, including those who speak Spanish, also speak English. I don't have to speak to them in Spanish because they'll speak to me in English."

She shook her head. "Languages open windows to a different culture."

"If I want to open a window to another culture I can always watch the Discovery Channel."

"You watch the Discovery Channel?"

"No, but I *could* is what I'm saying. It's on our basic cable package."

Renée put her hands over her eyes. For a split second I thought she was going to put her head down. Finally I could get some peace.

"Oh," she began, "then why are you speaking Swahili to people who you know speak English?"

"I was just trying to be polite, like you said. Don't you want me to be polite to people, show some manners and courtesy?"

"Of course I do!"

"Then why are you complaining?" I demanded.

"I'm not complaining, I was just wondering." She paused. "Has anybody ever told you that you can be incredibly frustrating?"

I got that from my teachers all the time. I was just pleased I was frustrating *her.*

"It wasn't like I was trying to learn Swahili," I said. "When I'm saying the words it's not even like I'm aware I'm speaking it. It just comes out."

"Do you know what a gift that is?"

"A gift would involve a nice box, a ribbon, and an expensive surprise inside," I said. "This is no big deal. You speak Swahili really well."

"Yes, but it took me a long time and—" She paused and gave me a confused look. "How do you know I speak really well?" she asked.

"You do, don't you?"

"Well, yes, but how do you know that?"

"It's not brain surgery. I watch the way people understand you, how fast you talk, the way you can make jokes. You even speak with the same accent as the local people."

Renée smiled. I liked her smile much more than her smirk.

"Do you know how I learned to speak Swahili?"

"Did I say something to suggest to you that I was psychic?"

She smirked. Maybe I did like her smirk. "I spent a year living in a Maasai community as part of a family."

"You lived in one of those mud huts?" I exclaimed.

She nodded. "I became a daughter and I lived with the family in their home."

"But . . . but . . . why?"

"I wanted to fully understand their lifestyle, their culture, their day-to-day existence."

"Wouldn't it have been easier to read some books and watch the Discovery Channel?"

"Easier, but not right. How can you hope to work with and help a community if you don't fully understand them?"

I didn't think she expected me to answer that question. Maybe she thought I'd be impressed. I guess I was, but not in the way she thought I would be. Who in their right mind would choose to live like that? Living like Ruth did . . . and her brothers and sisters, and her parents, and all of her relatives.

"You know, you're the only one on this trip who has been to a Maasai home."

"I am? Why just me?"

"We like people to experience things as we think they can handle them, but also as opportunities arise. Today just happened. Is that what's troubling you tonight, is that why you didn't want to eat?"

"Because I saw a girl living in a hut made of mud and cow dung who sleeps on the ground with her seven sisters in the same room with her four brothers and has to carry water for miles and just hope that it's clean and who spends her time cooking and cleaning and picking up after everybody, whose only dream is to go to school and half the time she can't go? Why would any of that bother me?"

She smiled, A soft, gentle smile.

"You, Alexandria, are an evolving surprise. I'm starting to think there might be something intelligent going on beneath that expensively clothed and well-groomed exterior."

"Again, I can't figure out if that's a sad attempt at a compliment or another thinly veiled shot."

"Take it as a compliment . . . and a warning."

"The compliment I don't need, but what do you mean by a warning?"

"Maybe that's the wrong word. I just need you to know that you have to do enough to make sure you graduate from this program, so the judge doesn't have a reason to order you into detention. I don't think detention would be good for you."

"That may be the first thing we both agree on. So, just write a good report."

"I can only write a truthful report. You're the only one who has control over what I'm going to write."

"You were right, 'warning' was the wrong word. Maybe 'blackmail' is the right one. Can I ask you a question?"

"Of course."

"Why do you treat me differently from everybody else?"

"I don't know what you mean," she said.

"Why do you treat everybody politely except for me?"

"I wasn't aware I was treating you any differently from—"

"Yes you are, and you know it!" I snapped.

She didn't answer right away. I could tell she was thinking, that she knew what I was saying was right. "I guess you are different from everybody else. You *are* the only one who's here against your will. You're the only one in the diversion program." She paused. "But maybe there's another reason."

"And what would that be?"

"Maybe you remind me a little bit of myself."

"A very little bit, I'm sure."

"You'd be surprised. I'm from a fairly well-off family. I had my share of difficulties with school, my parents, even brushes with the law. Maybe I see in you the potential to become more."

"By more, are you implying becoming *you?* Isn't that a little conceited on your part, to think that if I evolved and became better I might end up like *you?*"

"I certainly didn't—I didn't mean it that way," she stammered. "I'm sorry if that's the way it sounded."

"Well that *is* how it sounded. Or was that just something you were supposed to say to me . . . you tell me a little about your life, and somehow, through the magic of sharing, I break down in tears and tell you about my *terrible* life. How my parents don't really love me and instead they give me things to make up for their lack of time and love. Is that what you expect me to say? Well, my life isn't terrible. It's perfect, and once this ordeal is over I will go back to that perfect life. The only difference will be that I will appreciate it even more! Besides, I think I know *why* you like to treat me badly, why you seem to enjoy it so much."

"And why is that?"

"It makes you feel superior." I'd had enough of her and her attitude. Did she really think I was going to fall for any of this? Did she really think I was there to have her psychoanalyze me? I wasn't there to be some notch on her belt, to be another little life "saved." If she wanted to "Change The World" one person at a time, she wasn't going to start with me. I'd show her!

"Actually, that's the whole reason you do this for a living. You get to feel superior to *everybody*. Morally superior to the people who aren't here helping, and superior to the people you claim you're here to help. This is nothing more than one big, enormous ego trip, and you're mad at me because I see right through it."

I was surprised by the look on her face. She looked like she was going to cry. I'd expected to slap her, but I hadn't expected to stab her in the heart. For a split second I felt bad.

"You're wrong. You couldn't be more wrong if you tried."

"Really? Well, it doesn't matter. I'll do what I need to do to get through this, to satisfy the needs of my warden. In a few weeks I'll be gone and you can get on with your little drama. Now, if you have nothing more you want to lecture me about, I'm going to bed."

CHAPTER SIXTEEN

I held the handles tightly and made a run, forcing the wheel of the wheelbarrow to bump up the wooden ramp. I powered it up the ramp and into the building. There were people all around, holding shovels, waiting for the load of sand to mix with the cement. I dumped it in the middle of the floor and then turned away, trying to avoid the cloud of dust. I quickly retreated as—even worse—they dumped the bags of cement and dust billowed up into the air, into my lungs, and, worse, into my hair. I dragged the wheelbarrow backwards, getting out before the cloud could smother me.

"You're working hard," Renée said as I staggered out of the building, wheelbarrow in tow.

I nodded my head but didn't say anything. Those were the first words she'd said to me all day. I guess I'd really hurt her, either because what I'd said was way off base, or because my words had been too close to the truth for comfort.

Maybe both. But it didn't matter to me. I wasn't planning on saying anything to her. I'd just do the work I needed to do to make sure there was no way she could fail me. I wasn't going to leave her any room to hurt me back by sending me to jail.

I set the wheelbarrow down and Tim and Jimmy started filling it up again. I took a few steps away to avoid the dust and at least get out of the sun for a few seconds. In the distance, kids started coming out of the old school-house. I looked at my watch. It was about noon.

"Okay, everybody!" Renée called out. "I think that's our cue. Take a break for lunch!"

I didn't need to be told a second time. I walked over to the truck and grabbed my backpack. Inside was the lunch they'd packed for us. This was going to be another culinary delight, I was sure. I didn't have any choice about what I was going to eat, but I could choose who I was going to eat with.

I walked across the yard, among the school kids, looking for Ruth. I didn't have to look long. She saw me, waved, and a big smile bloomed across her face. She had such a beautiful smile, such perfect teeth, and I was pretty sure there was no orthodontist involved. She ran over and gave me a big hug.

"Can we have lunch together?" I asked.

Her smile got even bigger. "You sit under the big tree," she said, gesturing to it. "That's where the Standard Eight students sit. I'll get my lunch."

I walked toward the tree. I could see that it was the best spot in the whole yard, offering the biggest patch of shade. I had to chuckle. This wasn't so different from my school cafeteria, where everybody had a special spot and the coolest, most senior kids got the best location.

I settled into the dust with my back against the trunk. I unzipped my backpack and pulled out the paper bag. I guess this only made sense. I was working like some guy on a construction site, so why shouldn't I eat like the common man? Maybe I should learn to spit and whistle at pretty girls, too . . . that was what they did, wasn't it?

Ruth was the first of the girls to appear from the kitchen building. She was holding a bowl in her right hand and using the fingers of her free hand to eat from it as she walked. She settled down into the dirt beside me. I looked into her bowl. It was filled with white rice and some yellowish beans. It just might make my lunch look good.

I opened up the bag. An orange, already peeled, a bottle of water, and a pita, with . . . white rice and yellowish beans inside. *Sigh.*

"Do you want some orange?" I asked.

"Thank you."

She took the orange and pulled off a slice. She offered it to me. She then took a second section and passed the orange to another girl who had sat down beside her. We were now in the centre of half a dozen girls. That girl took a piece and handed it to the next girl. Soon the last slice was taken.

"Your hair," Ruth said. "It looks very . . . very . . . not as nice."

"That's being generous. My hair is *hideous.*"

"What is 'hideous'?"

"Terrible, awful, disgusting, like a witch."

"Witch?" she said, shaking her head. "You mean like sorceress, *kizee?* No, I wish *I* had hair like yours."

"And I wish I had cheekbones like yours," I said. "A lot of models would kill to have your facial structure. I can just imagine how pretty your eyes would look with makeup and . . . wait . . ." Maybe I didn't have to imagine.

I reached over, grabbed my backpack, and pulled out my makeup bag.

"Could I do your eyes?" I asked.

"Do what with them?"

I laughed. "Could I put on makeup, the colour and shading around my eyes?"

Ruth giggled. She said something to the other girls and they all started laughing.

"Yes," she said.

First I pulled out my eyeshadow. I opened the case and tried to decide which colour from the palette would be the best. I needed to do something that would complement her red uniform but also highlight her eye colour. I held her face in my hands and turned her head slowly. Her eyes were beautiful. They were a deep shade of brown with little flecks of gold. Gold, that was it, I'd play off the gold, but first I had to add some highlights.

I took the brush—my best Mac brush made of the finest of horsehair—and dabbed it against white. I ran the brush lightly underneath her eyebrows. She giggled and squirmed a little.

"Don't move or I won't be responsible for the outcome."

I applied another light coat. The white was very vibrant against her skin. I put the brush down. Next I needed an eyeliner. I rummaged among the dozen different eyeliners in the bag. I did a quick mental calculation— each was worth between twenty and forty dollars, so, on average, thirty dollars. That meant I had close to four hundred dollars' worth of eyeliner in there. What I didn't want to think about was what four hundred dollars would mean to these people.

So, which was the right eyeliner? I'd originally thought black, but realized that wouldn't provide contrast. Besides, unless you were an emo-kid, that was overdone and totally boring. I selected a brown one, from the Sephora line.

"Close your eyes and hold still."

I took the eyeliner and drew a thin line along the edge of the eyelid, as close to the lashes as possible. Very nice. I did the second eye. Funny, this was like working with a big Barbie doll—a big black Barbie doll. Didn't Barbie have a black friend? I couldn't remember her name, but I was pretty sure Malibu Barbie would have had a lot of trouble finding a black friend in Malibu.

The other girls all crowded in for a better look. They seemed fascinated by the process.

I picked up the brush again. It was time for the gold. I dabbed the brush, and in the space between the eyeliner and the white eyeshadow I applied a thicker coat of gold. I tried to be as gentle as I could. This was looking very good.

Next step, mascara. Her lashes were thick but I could make them thicker.

I put the eyeliner pencil back in the bag and selected my best mascara.

"Open your eyes really wide. This might tickle a bit."

I pulled out the applicator. As I brought it toward her eye she started to pull away.

"Stay still or I might accidentally poke you in the eye!"

She held tight and I started the top lashes. It went on very easily, but that was one of the benefits of top-of-the-line makeup.

Next I wanted to put on some concealer—did I have

anything that would match her skin? I looked at her face. There were no places where concealer was even needed. Her skin was even and blemish-free. How fair was that? Maybe living in a mud hut was like having a continual mud bath.

"There, you're done," I announced.

She opened her eyes. All the other girls started to laugh and smile and point and crowd all around.

"Here," I said. I pulled a mirror out of my bag and handed it to her.

She moved it around until she could see herself. Her smile got even bigger.

"I look . . . I look . . . *beautiful.*"

All the other girls laughed hysterically, and the boys came over and looked, and then the little girls who had been sitting elsewhere came running over to look as well. I backed away as Ruth became the centre of an ever-growing throng of kids.

Another girl—she looked as though she might be in Standard Eight too—tugged at my hand.

"Me next? Please?"

I couldn't help but smile. "Yes. You next."

Renée walked over to me. I started to get up off the ground. What was this all about? I'd just taken a lousy two-minute break from work, and now she was going to get all up in my face about it?

"It's okay, don't get up," she said.

I wasn't going to listen to anything she told me to do, so I did get up.

"You don't have to lecture. I'm ready to get back to work."

"No. that's okay. You deserve a break. You've been working very hard today. As hard as anybody here."

"I'm just doing what I have to do, that's all," I said.

"Alexandria, I know you're trying to make a point, but nobody is asking you to kill yourself. All this work must be hard on the nails."

I didn't know that she'd noticed. Even with work gloves, I'd busted off two nails on my right hand and a third on the left. I'd have them fixed first thing when I got back to civilization. Wait, was she being sarcastic?

"I'm actually here to extend an invitation to you," Renée said.

"An invitation from whom?"

"From one of the local chiefs. He wants you to come for supper."

"Why would he want *me* to come for supper?" I questioned suspiciously.

"I think it was the suggestion of his daughter, Ruth."

"Ruth's father is a chief? So that makes her like . . . like a princess," I gasped.

"They would just call her the chief's daughter, but that analogy works."

"I've never had a princess for a friend before."

"Neither has she," Renée said. "Sorry, that one *was* a shot."

"Calling me a princess isn't a shot. It's almost a compliment," I sniffed.

"The choice is yours, but you should know that it would be considered impolite for you not to accept."

I tried to think what supper would be like. Would we eat in their *castle,* that little hut made of mud and dung?

Could I stand the smoke in the air and the smell of cow dung? And what would they feed me?

"And you'd let me go?" I wasn't sure if I wanted her to say yes or no.

"I keep telling you, you're not in jail. You could leave with Ruth at the end of the day, and I'd send Nebala to get you at the village after supper to walk you home. If that's what you want?"

"I'm not dressed for company." I was wearing jeans today, of all things—okay, they were DKNY, but they were really filthy!

"I don't think they'll notice. So?"

My options were to go back with the others in the truck and eat what everybody else was going to eat—and it would be good and normal and nice—or go with Ruth and eat a mystery meal while squatting in the dirt.

"I'll go with Ruth."

"Good. Take along a bottle of water. You can eat whatever they cook, but whatever you do, don't drink the water, understood?"

"Don't worry about me. I'm not planning on drinking anything that doesn't come from a bottle."

We entered the village. It was still a muddy mess but somehow it didn't seem as bad, or as smelly, as I'd remembered it. Lots of ladies were sitting in front of their huts, but I didn't see Ruth's mother. I waited outside while Ruth and the rest of the kids ran into their home. Ruth quickly re-emerged.

"My mother is not feeling well. The baby is coming soon."

"Soon, like right now?" I gasped.

"Soon. A day or two, or a week. Soon."

Soon was good. Today, right now, was bad. Very bad.

"We have to get water," Ruth said.

I'd forgotten that having supper meant somebody, Ruth, had to fix that supper. It wasn't like she could just go to the refrigerator, or turn on a tap, or give an order to the household staff to prepare something. Maybe I *was* more of a princess than Ruth. My house certainly was a castle compared to hers. Actually, the cabana for our pool was more castle-like.

Ruth came out of the hut with two large yellow plastic canisters slung over her shoulders. She barked out an order—I could tell by the tone of her voice that it was an order even if I didn't understand the words. All of her sisters came out or stood up or walked over. Each grabbed a canister, including one little girl who was almost as small as the canister itself.

"Do you want to wait or come with us?" Ruth asked.

"Come with you." The alternative wasn't particularly pretty, or particularly pretty-smelling.

We made our way across the muddy field. I was super-careful not to step in anything other than mud. We left behind the corral and the fence and immediately swung to the right, away from the road and toward the hills. Up ahead were other girls also carrying brightly coloured water canisters. Some had them slung over a shoulder or on their backs. Some of the older girls had them balanced atop their heads.

It struck me then that it was just girls. Where were the boys? I didn't see any at first, and then I noticed some older boys walking beside us, but at a distance. Instead of carrying water canisters they all were holding spears.

"How come the boys don't have to carry water?" I asked.

"Not a boy job. They need to walk with spears."

"How is that going to help us get water?" This seemed so unfair. The girls were like pack animals and the boys just wandered around playing with weapons.

"Not help to carry, but help to get. *Askari.*"

"They're guarding us? From what?"

"The water hole isn't just for Maasai. For all the animals. Zebras, gazelles, antelopes. And where they go, lions follow."

I stopped dead in my tracks. Lions? Going for a walk in the heat and dust was one thing, but lions? Maybe I should have stayed with the smell, instead.

"These boys will protect us. Lions run when they see Maasai."

"But these are just boys!" I protested.

"You see boys. The lion sees Maasai. Don't fear."

Ruth took me by the hand and I walked away with her. The ground was rough and there were more trees and small mounds—big enough to hide a lion. In the near distance the hills were larger and covered with shrubs and bushes—big enough to hide an *elephant*. At least with an elephant I'd be able to see it coming and I could run. How fast could something that big move, anyway?

Ruth shrieked and jumped into the air, and I shrieked as well, shocked, struggling, looking all around. And then there was laughter. Her brother was standing a dozen steps behind us, and finally I realized why he was laughing. Lying on the ground right by Ruth's feet was a large chunk of dried-up cow dung. He'd hit her in the back with it. Ruth bent down, picked it up, and whipped it at him! It caught the side of his head with a glancing blow and shot past. Now all of the girls, including me, were laughing at him, and he didn't look nearly so amused.

"Can he really throw that spear?" I asked Ruth.

She yelled out to him and he trotted over, scowling and brushing the cow dung from his hair as he came. She said something else to him.

"I told him to hit the cactus," she explained.

He drew back his spear and threw it toward some cacti a dozen yards off to the side. The spear shot straight into the largest upright shoot, splitting it in two! He ran off proudly to retrieve his spear.

I didn't know whether I should be surprised, impressed, or just feel a little bit safer. What I did know was that I was really glad he'd only thrown a cow pie at us.

There was a definite downward slope to the land. We were headed toward a little gully. I could see the bottom, where it started to slope up on the other side, but I couldn't make out even a thin line of water down there. Soon we were walking on what had obviously once been the river. Loose sand shifted underfoot, and I could see a high-water mark on the side of the rocks. This was, during the rainy season, I guessed, a wide, fast-moving river. Now it was all dried up . . . all dried up except for some muddy spots in the middle . . . and there were kids standing in the mud . . . no, that couldn't be right . . . they were filling up their water containers from the water in the mud puddles!

I stumbled forward, swept along by the wave of kids carrying canisters. The mud puddle was at the bottom of a trough, a depression that had been dug into the sand. It wasn't much bigger than a backyard pool. There were two girls at the bottom. As they filled each container they passed it up the slope to another girl, who passed it up higher until it reached the flat, sandy bottom. I watched as they filled a dozen containers. The water looked dark and dirty. It *was* dark and dirty. How could it be anything else?

The first group of girls finished filling all their containers and climbed out of the depression. Two of Ruth's sisters, including one who couldn't have been any older than four or five, climbed down to the bottom, and the older girls tossed and rolled all the containers down to them. Other sisters went partway down the slope and Ruth and I stayed at the top. The littlest girl tilted the container into the puddle and it quickly filled. She handed it up. I could see the strain in her face, see the muscles of her arms working to hold it up. Hand to hand, the container made it to the top, where Ruth took it and placed it down in the sand between us. The water was filthy! They couldn't use this for cooking or for washing, and it certainly wasn't anything that they could even think about drinking.

A second and then a third container made it to the top.

"This water . . . it doesn't look very clean," I said.

"Not now. It has to sit so the dirt falls to the bottom."

"And that makes it clean?"

"Not clean, but clean enough to use. Oh, look!" Ruth said, and she pointed to the rocks off to one side.

Peeking around the rocks and ridge was what seemed like a whole herd of animals. There were zebras and some little gazelles and a couple of impalas.

"They're waiting their turn," Ruth said. "They'll drink after we leave."

"But how can they all drink from this?"

"In small groups. They'll take turns. It's maybe the only water around here," she answered.

Then I remembered something I'd read. "If there are grazing animals like that, doesn't that mean there are animals around who will try to eat them?"

"There will be, but not now. See how calm they are," she said.

They did look calm, quiet, gentle, almost like little pets, patiently waiting for us to finish. Then I caught movement out of the corner of my eye. I felt a rush of fear and then realized it was just two of Ruth's brothers and another boy. They were circling around the herd. I guess they wanted to get a closer look or . . . no, not a closer look . . . they wanted to get close enough to kill one of the animals.

I watched as the three boys moved, slowly, from rock to rock, or just froze in place, moving slowly again as the herd stared in a different direction.

"They are trying to move downwind," Ruth explained. "Most animals smell better than they see."

I was mesmerized. I had never seen anything hunted before, never seen anybody hunting. I was a meat-eater, but I'd never seen a living animal become meat before my eyes. Part of me was cheering the boys on, and part of me was almost panic-stricken and thought I should yell out to warn the animals. These were a bunch of cute little animals. Wasn't this like trying to kill Bambi?

The boys got closer and closer . . . and the herd suddenly bolted! The boys ran after them and tossed their spears, which flew through the air and landed harmlessly in the dirt where the animals had just been. They'd all gotten away. Again, I wasn't sure whether I should be disappointed or cheer.

"That is the last of them," Ruth said.

The girls all picked up containers.

"Here, let me help," I said, offering to relieve Ruth of one of her burdens.

"No, you are a guest."

"It would be rude if you didn't allow me to help," I said.

Ruth nodded her head. She lowered one of her containers to the ground—the littler of the two. I picked it up by the strap. It weighed a ton! It banged against my leg as I struggled forward.

"Easier if you carry it different," Ruth said.

She took it from me, looped the strap over my head, and put the container on my back. "Hold the strap with both hands and rest around your head."

She helped me get it into position. It was still heavy, but at least the weight was now distributed between my back, my hands, and my head. Maybe this way I could do it, or at least get it partway back. I struggled up the little slope.

Beside me was one of Ruth's little sisters. She was carrying a container identical to mine, the same size exactly, using the same method Ruth had shown me. She was probably seven, maybe eight years old. She looked over at me and smiled. If she could do it, there was no way I could put that container down.

CHAPTER SEVENTEEN

I drank the last of the water from my bottle. It helped to wash down the cornmeal mush that had been the basis of our supper—that and some beans and a little bit of rice. Because Ruth's father had invited me, I had assumed that he would be joining us for the meal, but he hadn't appeared. None of the men had. They were all still out with the cattle, and it was the women and children who ate together, carefully saving enough food for the men for later.

The strange food had made me nervous at first, but I'd watched Ruth and her sisters cook it all. I'd even helped . . . a bit. It certainly wasn't *haute cuisine* but it wasn't bad, either. The worst part was having to squat around the little table while we ate. It was a far cry from sitting in our dining room with fine china, a freshly ironed linen table-cloth, my grandmother's antique sterling silver, candles lit, classical music playing discreetly in the background, with half a dozen courses prepared by the cook and served to us. A different world, for sure.

Funny, though, I had few memories of smiles around our own dining-room table, and I couldn't even imagine my family spontaneously breaking into song. But these people were just like that, and I couldn't understand why they seemed so happy. They had nothing . . . and they were *happy.* How was that even possible? How happy would they have been if they'd had everything we had? Utterly ecstatic, right? Or would any of it have made a real difference? Was it possible it would even have made them *less* happy? It was kind of hard for me to get my head around.

All around us other families had been having supper together the same way. It was as though we were separate but together. And there were so many kids. Every home was overflowing with children. I knew some families with two kids, usually one of each, a boy and a girl . . . what did they call that, *a millionaire's family?* That wasn't true because most of the millionaires I knew believed in the *one-and-done* theory of children. More than half of my friends were only children, squeezed in between their parents' work and social and charitable commitments. It wasn't that they couldn't afford to have a lot more children, but they couldn't afford the *time* to have more. One was essential, and possibly a second was good—you know, like an heir and a spare—but anything more was deemed superfluous. Interestingly, they didn't consider having too many cars or too big a house or too much money to be unnecessary, but extra kids were not considered.

There were times with some of my friends when I got the feeling that they were more like accessories than children. Their parents trotted them out, showed them off, and then pushed them into the background to be raised by surrogate parents and placated by cars and cash and activities. I had to admit it, sometimes I felt a little bit that way too.

"There are so many children," I said to Ruth.

"Many."

"And is one of them your best friend?" I asked.

"They are all friends."

"But is one your very *best* friend?"

She looked confused.

"You know, somebody you want to spend time with the most, the person you like talking to, that you want to do things with . . . your *best* friend?"

She nodded and smiled and then pointed at me. "You. You are my best friend."

"Me?" I gasped. "But there has to be somebody else."

"I like everybody, but I want to spend time with you. Do you have a best friend?"

I instantly thought of the girls I hung around with, the ones I shopped with, went to school with. There were so many, but not one name popped out. I had friends, but did I have a best friend?

I pointed at Ruth. "You. You are *my* best friend."

Her smile became even broader and she gave me a big hug. I guess in part I had said it for the same reason you have to say "I love you" when somebody says it to you first, but there was more. Ruth felt like the first person I'd met in a whole long time who wasn't trying to impress me, or who I didn't have to try to impress. I got the feeling I could tell her anything and she'd hold on to that secret and not use it as a juicy tidbit the next time she was talking to somebody. I didn't know if I knew anybody else I could say that about.

I heard a gentle ringing and realized what it was.

Some of the cows had bells. The cows were coming
home, the fathers were coming home with their herds.
Almost instantly the first cows poked their heads through
the small opening in the wall that ran around the village
and strolled into the corral. It was as if somebody had
turned on a tap. They just kept coming and coming, until
they began to fill the large muddy pasture.

"There are a lot of cows," I said.

"Many," Ruth said. "Our village has many. My father
has many. How many cows does your family have?"

"We don't have any."

"Oh, that is so sad," she said, and she did look gen-
uinely sorry for me.

"We're not Maasai," I explained. "We don't keep cows.
We keep cars and money."

"Aahhhh."

Apparently that made sense to her.

"We don't have cows because we know that all the
cows in the world belong to the Maasai and it would be
rude of us to keep your cattle."

Ruth laughed. "I will tell my father that. That will
make him laugh."

"Your father must be coming soon," I said.

"Maybe, but maybe not. Depends on where the herd
was today."

"I'd like to meet him. Hopefully I can wait around
until he comes."

"I do not think so. Look."

Among the cattle were a number of men, and I recognized one—it was Nebala. He'd come to get me.

"I guess my ride is here." I gave Ruth a hug. "Could
you please say 'Asante sana' to your mother for me?" Her
mother had gone inside to lie down. She wasn't feeling

well. I guess she was proof that being pregnant didn't necessarily get easier just because you had a lot of practice.

I waved goodbye to the other girls and made my way across the pasture. It was harder now. It wasn't just cowpies I had to dodge but cows. They were everywhere. I know, it was Africa, so it should have been lions and leopards that I was afraid of, but cut me some slack—these cows were big and they had horns and—

"Uhhh!" I lifted up my foot. I'd stepped in a fresh, heaping, still-steaming pile of cow crap. I shook my foot and a few little flecks came off, while a couple of shaken pieces bounced off my leg! Like *that* was somehow better!

I limped over to Nebala.

"Look before you leap," he said. "Old African saying."

"Right. Just get me home and I'll change my shoes." And my clothes, and shampoo my hair, and put on some fresh makeup. Then I thought how I hadn't even met Ruth's father. I wanted to meet him. "Could we stay a little longer?"

"We do not have time. We have to leave now."

"Just a few more minutes, please?" I said, putting on my best puppydog face.

"No. We need to leave now. There is only so much light."

"But it's not going to be dark for a while, and so what if we're in the truck after . . ." Then it came to me. "Did you bring the truck?"

"I brought my feet," he said. "Left and right."

"You mean we're walking?"

"We could beam you up . . . Scotty."

"Funny." *Star Trek* was officially getting old.

"Then we walk. Or we could run. Maasai can run without stopping."

"I'm not Maasai, so we'll have to settle for walking. I'm sorry you had to come all this way to get me."

"I like walking."

"So do I, but it's still nice of you. *Asante*."

"*Karibu*."

"Is this your village?" I asked as we started to walk, wondering if he was related to Ruth.

"Not even my clan. My village is in that direction," he said, pointing off toward some distant hills.

"How far is it?"

"Depends. Maybe five hours if I walk without stopping."

"How far is that?"

"Five hours."

"No, I meant distance. How many miles is it?"

He shook his head. "I don't know. I just know how long it is from here to there. Five hours."

I looked at my watch. It was almost five-thirty. The sun went down at about six-thirty and there was a dusk that followed for another twenty minutes or so. We had to travel another two and a half miles in the next hour and a bit. Moving at this pace, we could do it. That was good. With or without a Maasai warrior, I didn't want to be out here in the dark.

The road was, as always, potholed and grooved and washed out. The scenery was the only thing that changed. Sometimes we passed fields of cultivated corn. Other places the vegetation was sparse, with only a few cacti and the occasional tree or a couple of shrubs. From time to time the road banked around small bumps of hills or passed by rocky outcrops. There were villages off in the distance sometimes, with little pillars of smoke rising up into the sky from the centre. There were also some of the roadside stands I'd seen before, small shacks where people sold their wares. They were all closed for the night.

As the sun was starting to fade it cast longer shadows, and my mind started to play tricks with the shadows, wondering what might be hidden behind every object.

"Do you ever get spooked when you're out here alone?" I asked.

"'Spooked'?" he said, shaking his head. "What means 'spooked'?"

"Nervous, scared."

He laughed. "I am Maasai. There is nothing in the world that frightens me. Nothing."

"Come on, everybody is afraid of something. High places, public speaking, dogs, snakes—" He made a little sound when I said "snakes." "Are you afraid of snakes?"

"Not afraid. I just do not like them. Snakes are so, so, creepy."

I had to laugh. I hated snakes too.

I went to put my foot down and then saw something in the road and stepped to the side. It was a gigantic piece of cow dung, so big that if I had stepped in it my shoe would have sunk in all the way up to my ankle.

Nebala squatted down beside the cow-pie. What in the world was he doing? He was examining the crap! Obviously I wasn't the only one who was amazed by the size of it.

"That must be from the biggest cow in the entire world," I said.

"Not cow. Elephant."

"Elephant . . . an *elephant* was here?"

He touched his foot against it and a little bit of steam rose into the air. "A minute or two ago."

Anxiously I looked all around. I couldn't see an elephant. I couldn't even see a place where an elephant might be hiding. Unless it was behind those bushes, or maybe it had circled around the hill, or what about the cornstalks? No, they weren't as tall as an elephant's eye. Great, I was looking for an elephant in Kenya and I was quoting lines from last year's school play, *Oklahoma!*

Nebala tilted back his head and inhaled deeply through his nose. What did he hope to smell except the huge pile of elephant dung at his feet? He turned his head all around, looking in all directions, smelling the air. Was he trying to smell the elephant?

He took me by the hand. "Come," he said quietly.

I wanted to ask him what he saw, or what he smelled, but I didn't seem to have any words. I let him lead me off the road and into the cornstalks. He put his finger to his lips to indicate silence and we wove slowly between the stalks, trying not to rustle them as we passed. It felt good to be off the road . . . but what else might be hiding in the cornstalks with us?

Nebala motioned for me to get lower.

"Stay," he said, and he started to move away before I grabbed him.

"Where are you going?" I hissed.

He motioned with his hand that he was going to circle around.

"Is there an elephant?" I whispered.

He shook his head. "Listen."

"I don't hear anything."

"Not elephant. *Elephants.*"

He started to move again and I grabbed him by the arm.

"What do I do if they come when you're gone?"

"Drop to your knees."

I nodded my head. "Right, I get it, I should get low so they won't see me."

"No, always good to be on your knees when you pray to your God."

"No, seriously."

"Seriously. Here." He took his spear and stuck it in the ground.

"But won't you need that?"

"Elephants," was his one-word response, and I understood. What good was a spear against an elephant?

I released his arm and he started off, angling away from the road, moving through the cornstalks. I tried to follow his path, peering through the stalks, catching little glimpses of him until I couldn't see him any more. I turned back in the other direction and tried to see past the corn to the road. I really couldn't see anything. I didn't like that. I needed to see what was happening. I needed to do something instead of just squatting in the cornstalks, quaking and waiting.

Dropping to my knees I crawled along the ground, moving toward the road. If I peeked out I could at least see what was happening. I trusted Nebala, but really, how could a herd of elephants be there without me hearing or seeing them? I was sure they were someplace, maybe a mile away, and he was just trying to be super-careful.

I was almost at the edge of the field. Soon I'd be able to look down the road and—a gigantic leg appeared, followed by another and another and another. I froze in place as a second set of legs, as thick as tree trunks, and almost close enough for me to reach out and touch, glided by me. How could anything that big move that quietly and quickly? I tried to look up, following the legs, but I was blocked by the stalks—thank *goodness* I was blocked.

They'd passed by. They were heading down the road,

away from me. I was safe now. Unbelievable, a herd of elephants had just passed right by me! At least, I'd seen their legs pass by. I hadn't actually seen all of them. I knew I shouldn't. I knew it was stupid and probably dangerous, but I couldn't resist. I had to look.

I crawled, this time even more slowly, until I could look out. There, moving down the road, were four elephant butts—one of them a baby butt. Cute. He couldn't have been any bigger than a compact car. I wished I'd had a camera with me because nobody was ever going to believe this.

One of the elephants, the last in line, suddenly stopped and spun around. It turned its head slightly to the side as though it was trying to listen, or look. Was it looking at me? And those two big ears started flapping. Was I making any sounds other than my breathing? Could those big ears have picked up the sound of my breath, or my heart, which felt like it was pounding through my chest?

There was a loud scream and I had to fight the urge to jump or scream back. The elephant turned around, away from me. There was something down the road, a flash of red—it was Nebala! He was fifty yards down the road. He was standing in the middle, visible to me and certainly visible to the elephants, waving his arms and hooting so there was no way they could miss him.

The elephants stood still, staring at him. What was he doing? And what were the elephants thinking? Were they as confused as I was? Then, without warning, they charged toward him! A pounding, the thundering of feet throwing up dust! And they trumpeted as they ran! I saw Nebala dodge one way and then the other, scrambling back into another section of the corn that hid me!

I fought the urge to stand and run up the road, away from the elephants and toward the compound, but I couldn't do that. I had to wait. I had to go back to the spot where Nebala had left me, the place where he'd be coming back to get me . . . if he *could* come back. I started to scramble back before I realized that I wasn't necessarily going in the right direction. All the stalks looked the same, and it wasn't like they were even planted in rows.

I had to slow down. I took a deep breath. I needed to settle my heart rate. I took another breath. Complete silence. The wind wasn't even rustling the corn. How could it go from so loud to so quiet? The elephants must have kept running, far away, away from Nebala. Or else they'd squashed him like a bug and were now quietly doubling back to get me.

That was just crazy. Elephants didn't stalk people . . . I had to stop thinking about that and start just *thinking*. I *had* to think.

Maybe all the stalks looked the same but not all of them surrounded a Maasai spear stuck in the ground. I just had to find the spear. It would be good to have that spear in my hands. Not that it would stop an elephant, but it could stop other things . . . other things that might be hiding among the stalks with me. Again, I had to smarten up, stop letting my imagination run away with me. On the other hand, I *was* in Africa—was it really so crazy to worry about a lion or a spitting cobra here? It wasn't like I was worried about a street gang or getting hit by a truck or—

I heard a rattle, a shifting in the cornstalks. I froze in place. There was no point in running because pretty much anything I was worried about could for sure outrun me. My only hope was to stay perfectly still and hope it wouldn't see me . . . or hear me . . . or smell me. God, how did I stop myself from emitting an odour?

"You moved."

I practically jumped into the air. It was Nebala. And he was holding his spear.

"I told you not to move."

"Elephants," I said. "There were elephants."

"I told you there were elephants. Did you think I was wrong?"

"Not wrong. I just needed to see for myself."

He shook his head. "Maasai women and white women all must see for themselves. Just *believe* sometimes."

"Shouldn't we be quiet?"

"Elephants are gone."

"But they were right there."

He shook his head. "Far away. No danger."

"I *saw* them. I saw *you*."

He looked surprised.

"I saw what you did. You made them chase you. How did you get away?"

"I ran."

"You're faster than an elephant?"

He laughed. "I ran like this," he said, and he swerved his arm back and forth in a zigzag motion. "Elephants don't turn well and they don't chase long. They just wanted me to go away, and I *wanted* to go away, so we both wanted the same thing."

"I can't believe it. You were chased by a herd of elephants," I said, shaking my head in disbelief. "That had to be terrifying."

"I am *Maasai*." He fixed me with a fierce look.

"Come on, be honest."

His fierce face dissolved into a smile. "Maybe a little scared." Then he laughed, and all the tension I'd been feeling fell away. "But that's just our secret."

He gave me the Vulcan salute and I returned it.

CHAPTER EIGHTEEN

I tried to be the first off the truck. I wanted to drop over, poke my head in the door of Standard Eight, and say hello to Ruth. I knew the teacher wouldn't mind if I just said hello. They probably wouldn't have had time to start a test this morning, and even if they had, it wasn't like I was going to disrupt them too much. I wanted to tell Ruth all about the elephants. I needed to tell somebody, and Nebala had made me promise not to tell anybody at the centre. Half of the kids would have been scared, and the other half would probably have wanted to go out looking for them! Telling Ruth would be different. I knew she wouldn't tell anybody else if I asked her not to. I knew I could trust her.

The door was open and I could hear them. The teacher was saying something and the whole class was reciting back what he had said. I hadn't seen a lot of their class but this was one of the patterns I'd noticed. Memorizing things was a big part of their day. Memorizing and then repeating and then writing what they'd memorized and repeated in examinations.

What a strange concept. Having to write a test to see if they'd *let* you go to high school. And then, if you got the marks, hoping that you had enough money to go, and walking miles and miles every day before you went home and did all your chores and tried to grab enough daylight to study some more. I knew some people who wouldn't go to the end of their driveway without being driven. In fact, I *was* one of those people.

And I thought about how many of my friends cut class or complained about what a waste it was to go to school, or how bad and boring it was, or gave their teachers a hard time. Again, sometimes that was me.

I peeked my head in. They all stopped, looked at me, laughed, and pointed. So much for being unobtrusive.

"I was looking for Ruth . . . I don't see her."

"She is away today," the teacher said.

"Does anybody know why?" I asked.

One of the girls in the corner raised her hand. I recognized her. She lived in Ruth's village. She was a cousin.

The teacher motioned for her to speak. "She is home, helping. The baby will come today. She will help."

That was so exciting! And scary. Ruth could fix meals and gather water, but she couldn't be expected to deliver a baby, could she? They had to have a doctor or nurses.

"There will be many helpers," the teacher said. I think he was reading my worried expression. "Women who are *very* experienced. Midwives who deliver babies." He smiled. "There have been many babies in the village. No need to worry."

I appreciated him saying all that, but I was still going to worry. Maybe babies happened all the time here, but not in my life, and when they did happen there were big, sanitary hospitals staffed with doctors and nurses all ready to help with drugs and instruments and delivery rooms and operating rooms and whatever was needed. Here, there was just mud and dust. What if something went wrong? I couldn't think about that.

I heard the rumble of wheelbarrows being rolled along the rutted ground, the clang of shovels and trowels being thrown down from the truck. My prison work day was starting, and pretty soon I knew I'd hear my own personal warden.

I decided I'd better let the students get on with their studying, For now, I had some work of my own to get to.

I felt dirty and grungy. My hair was disgusting. I was filthy. Covered in dirt, mud, and cement powder, with sprinkles of plaster stuck to my skin. To top it all off, I could feel pain in muscles I hadn't even known I had. Altogether, though, I didn't feel terrible. I felt sort of neutral, nothing, almost numb. Maybe the whole working hard thing had put me in a state of shock, and that's why I wasn't feeling miserable, the way I should. This was sort of an out-of-body experience. I was suffering a hideous fashion death, and yet I was hovering above, looking down at the corpse, trying to decide if I should go to the light, or return . . . or have a shower.

My way of dealing with all the worry about Ruth's mother was to just lose myself in the work. I couldn't help her or the baby but I could help to build a school that the new little baby would go to some day. A school

that was made of more than mud and barbed wire, a
school where the baby could learn, and grow . . . if there
was enough money.

"Is there any hot water left at all?" I asked as Mary
Beth came out of the shower.

"Maybe not hot, but at least sort of warm. I tried not
to take too much." She sounded guilty.

"That's okay," I said. "I know you weren't in there very
long."

I closed the door behind me. I laid out my fresh, new
clothes on the bench. It would feel good to get into something clean. I stripped out of my clothing. There were bits
of mud and plaster ground into every little nook and
cranny and crevice of my body. This wasn't going to be
fast. How many people were still in line behind me? Two
or three. I didn't care of it was twenty-two or thirty-three.
I needed to get myself clean. I'd need to take a much
longer shower than Mary Beth had, but that only made
sense—I had five times the hair she had and twenty times
the need to look good.

I started the water. It wasn't hot, but it was warm
enough. I let the water work its way through my hair. At
first it just seemed to run off, repelled by the cement dust,
which had formed a waterproof seal over my hair. I took
some shampoo and lathered it up. I could feel the grit
against my fingers and scalp. It felt awful. I rinsed it out,
trying to get all the last bits of dust and dirt and shampoo
out. I'd just do it another time or two and I'd be certain to
get it all out.

I tipped the bottle slightly, filling my hand with shampoo. Then I stopped. I really didn't need to do it again, and
there was no guarantee that the warm water wouldn't turn
to cold in the middle, leaving me with a lathery mess on

my head. And there were two people still waiting. I'd just soap up, finish up, and get dressed. And then eat. I was hungry like I never remembered being hungry before. I wondered who was cooking the meal tonight at Ruth's. Were they celebrating a new baby in the family, or were they grieving a loss? I didn't know, and there was no way I could find out right now. I'd just have to wait.

"Are you sure you don't want to come along?" Sarah asked. She'd come to my tent to try to talk me into it.

"I'm sure."

They were all going to be part of a ceremony that night at a Maasai village. This was to be their first experience. For me, I was too preoccupied to want to go. The only village I cared about was Ruth's. I'd just wait here. Wait and worry.

"I just want to rest up my back so I'll be able to work tomorrow," I said. This was really an excuse, although there was some truth to it. I'd pulled a muscle in my back somewhere between pushing the wheelbarrow and shovelling concrete. Hard to imagine anyone back home believing me if I told them that I'd hurt myself that way. I was sure they couldn't picture me doing either of those things. Heck, I'd done them, and even *I* could hardly picture it.

"You'll miss out on the fun."

"I'll be just fine here. I have a book to read, and I'll get to bed early."

"They also said we might see animals along the way. Apparently this is the best time to see them, just after dusk. I'm hoping for some elephants."

"Be careful what you wish for."

"I know, but it's not like there are actually any elephants anywhere around here."

I almost laughed out loud, but stopped myself.

"Everything will be all right," Sarah said, as she put a hand on my shoulder.

She was sweet. In some ways she reminded me of Ruth. At least, she reminded me more of Ruth than she did anybody back home. Sarah could be a friend too. And Mary Beth. I could just imagine the looks on the faces of my friends back home if the four of us went walking through the mall together. They'd think I had lost my mind entirely. Well, I'd certainly lost something. And gained something else.

"Do you think you could do me a favour?" Sarah asked.

"Depends on the favour."

"I'm almost embarrassed to ask." She did look kind of uncomfortable. "It's just that I've never been much for makeup, and I saw what you did for Ruth. And I was just wondering . . . do you think that . . . if it isn't too much trouble . . . if you could . . ."

"Do your makeup?"

She nodded her head and looked down at her feet.

"I could, but I have to warn you, it might lead to trouble."

"Trouble?"

"Yeah, you might have Tim chasing you around the compound."

She giggled and blushed.

"Why don't you see if Mary Beth wants her makeup done, too."

—

"I'm out of here." Christina had run in after her shower, but just to grab a pen and a notebook to take with her. Was it something I said?

"You don't want a makeover?" I asked her. "I'm offering a special today for cosmetics newbies. I promise I won't stab you with my eyeliner." Okay, maybe that was a bit mean, because I really didn't have a problem with her if she didn't have a problem with me. But she just scowled at me and muttered something about "better things to do" with her time and took off.

I took my book to the dining room, where I settled into a chair with a cup of steaming chai tea. Everybody else was at the far side of the compound in their tents, getting ready, and it was almost quiet—a little taste of what it was going to be like when I was alone. It was going to be just me and the *askari*. The only other person in the dining room now was Renée.

She was the last person I wanted to see. Partly because of how she'd been treating me and the things she'd said. I wasn't sure which made me more upset—the things that weren't true or the things that were.

Just as upsetting to me was the way I'd treated her. She wasn't a bad person, and I really hadn't believed most of what I'd said to her. I'd been angry, and I'd said things to hurt her. Words were sometimes hard to take back. It wasn't like returning something you didn't like to the store. It wasn't as if you could get store credit. Or any credit. Renée probably didn't want to talk to me any more than I wanted to talk to her.

So I sat at one end of the deck, pretending to read, and she sat at the other end. Who knows, maybe she actually was reading. All around us was the gathering dark. The night was closing in. Soon I wouldn't be able to see more than a dozen feet beyond the haze of the dining-room lights. I looked forward to that. In the darkness I could look up and see a billion stars, twinkling and glittering. Sure, they were the same stars I could see in the same sky at home, but here there were no street lights or house lights or any lights, so I could actually see them. Here there were only the three bulbs hanging from the rafters of the dining area, powered by the generator. I could hear it humming away in the distance. If I'd really wanted to, I could have used the electricity to power my hair-straightener and make my hair look really good. But really, who was I trying to impress? And did anything like that really impress anybody, anyway? Better to just sit here and read.

I looked over at Renée. I didn't know what she was reading but she was really into that book. She looked up at me and I quickly looked away, embarrassed that I'd been caught looking. Maybe she hadn't seen me, or . . . she stood up and came walking toward me. She stood overtop of me.

"I guess I owe you an apology," she said.

"For what?"

"You've worked harder today than everybody else here."

"Not everybody," I said. "I've watched you work."

"Me? That's my job. I get paid. The rest of you are volunteers . . . well, almost all of you . . . and I don't mean that as a shot."

"I know."

She sat down on a chair right across from me.

"Can I ask you a question?" I said.

"Of course."

"I was noticing. It isn't just me you give a hard time to. There's also Christina. You're pretty hard on her sometimes, as well."

Renée smirked. There was that look. "I guess I am sometimes. I think it's because the two of you have so much in common."

"Us? We have absolutely nothing in common!"

"Sure you do. You can both be pretentious princesses."

"I am *not* a pretentious . . . not all the time. But what's that got to do with her?"

"She uses her knowledge and education the same way you use your money and background. It keeps people in their place, puts her above everybody and everything. You can't be *with* the people and *above* the people at the same time. It took me a while to realize that, although I guess I still need a reminder from time to time myself."

"I really didn't mean that. I was just angry."

"You *were* angry, but you *did* mean it, and I appreciated you being that honest with me. We're all here to learn from each other. I've learned from you."

"Seriously? What have you learned from me?"

"Not to be prejudiced."

"I can't even imagine you being prejudiced against anybody." She treated everybody—black or white, young or old—the same way.

"My prejudice was that I saw you, all blond and made-up and rich, and assumed you'd be stupid and snooty and a royal pain in the butt."

"And?"

"And you were never stupid," she said, and smirked.

"Just snooty and a pain, right?"

She nodded. I wasn't going to argue the point.

"I have great hopes for Christina," Renée said. "I think she's grown through this experience. I might even offer her a job one day."

"And me?" I asked.

"I have even higher hopes. There's a saying: From those to whom much is given, much is expected. You have so much—and I'm not talking about money—so you have a lot to give. Don't let anybody sell you short." She reached out and touched my hand. "Especially not yourself."

Ever so slightly I nodded my head. I knew what she meant. I even agreed with what she meant. But that didn't mean I could follow through. The hardest person to overcome, I thought, is yourself.

"You have so much going inside your head—things that you don't even like to admit to yourself," Renée said.

"Such as?"

"Your gift for languages, for one."

I shrugged. "I'm okay with them, I guess."

"You're more than okay. And the way you can figure out numbers."

"I suppose shopping does train you for something," I joked.

"Yeah, but it's not just dollars. I heard you talking to the other kids about bags of cement and weights and numbers of blocks. You have an amazing ability with figures."

Again I shrugged. I had always been good at math, but for the most part the only figure that mattered to me was my own, and the only number was my weight or the amount in my wallet.

"And," Renée continued, "I also know what a kind heart you have. Not just with Ruth. That was so nice of you to do Sarah and Mary Beth's makeup. Did you see the way the boys were looking at them? It was priceless."

"It was fun."

"Do you think you might stay in touch with them when you get home?" Renée asked.

"They live halfway across the country from me."

"You're right. It's too bad we don't have the techno-logical magic to miraculously reach out electronically across the globe—oh, wait a minute, we do! It's called the Internet."

"A do-gooder *and* a comedian?"

"And how about Ruth?"

"I didn't see a computer in her hut," I said.

"But there is one in our offices in Nairobi. You could send her messages or mail and I'd make sure she gets it. That is, if you want to stay in contact."

"I do. I really do."

"Excellent. The royal connection. The Maasai princess and the California princess! Sorry, that's my last shot!"

"No offence taken, although you could make it up to me," I said.

"What did you have in mind?"

I reached down and picked up my purse. I opened it up and pulled out my makeup bag.

"Noooo," she said, shaking her head.

"Why not?"

"I just don't wear makeup, that's all."

"Again, why not?"

"I just don't."

"Are you so afraid that if people see you with makeup on they won't be able to see beneath the makeup to realize that people can have eye makeup but still see clearly? Or that they can have beautiful hair but still have beautiful minds? Or that they can have fashion but not be defined by anybody's prejudicial ideas about clothes or—"

"Okay, okay, you win!" she exclaimed, holding her hands above her head in surrender. "Besides, maybe I'd just like to see how good I can look."

She threw her arms around me and gave me a big hug. I used one arm to hug her back. What the heck, I put down my makeup bag and wrapped my other arm around her too.

"Okay, let's stop now before this leads to a group hug," I said.

"No group hug, but are you sure you don't want to join in the group activity?"

"I'm fine. I'll enjoy being here by myself. Besides . . . there's my sore back."

"Doesn't surprise me. You've probably been working harder than you ever have in your entire life."

"Not probably. Definitely." I paused. "Working hard enough to pass through the program?"

"Not probably. Definitely. Just out of curiosity, your back isn't the only reason you're not going, is it? You're worried about Ruth and her mother."

"Aren't you?"

"I'm thinking about them, but I'm not worried. People give birth here all the time. They don't seem to need hospitals and doctors."

"Ever?"

"Well . . . hardly ever."

"It's the *hardly ever* I'm worried about."

"Probably everything is already fine. You'll get the good news tomorrow," Renée said.

"Then tomorrow I'll stop worrying."

"Okay. I'd better get myself ready. Are you okay to be here on your own? I could stay to keep you company."

"They need you to translate."

"I could leave another staff member," she suggested.

"That wouldn't be fair to them. Besides, it's not like I'm going to be completely alone. There are the *askari.*"

"They'll keep you safe."

"And I promise not to invite anybody over for a wild party while you're all away. So, enough talking, and let me do your makeup."

CHAPTER NINETEEN

I was startled out of my thoughts by a loud, long ringing. It sounded like a gigantic doorbell. I wanted to ask what it was but there was nobody to ask. There was only me, a fire for company, and the *askari* out by the fence. Actually, I hadn't even seen them. They moved so silently through the darkness that they were almost invisible when they were on patrol.

The bell rang again.

"Isn't somebody going to get that?" I yelled out into the night to nobody in particular.

It rang a third time. This time it went on and on and on—and then stopped. There was silence, except for the humming of the generator and the chirping of crickets.

I waited for it to ring again, but there was nothing. Whatever it was, whoever it was, they'd gone away. I could get back to my book and my tea and my worries. I just wished I knew that everything was okay with Ruth.

An *askari* stepped out of the darkness right in front of me and nearly scared me out of my sandals. He was very young, not much older than me. Most of the *askari,* with the exception of some of the leaders like Nebala, were young.

"You need to come," he said.

"Me? Why? What do you want?"

"Come."

He started walking away into the darkness. I jumped up, slung my bag over my shoulder, and ran to catch up to him. He had that typical Maasai walk, a long, bouncy stride that covered a lot of ground.

"What's wrong?" I demanded. "Where am I going?"

He didn't answer. He led me around the dining hall, through the thicket, along the path. We rounded a corner and I could see the front gate—it was open. There were two other *askari* standing there. Alongside them were some people and . . . was that a wheelbarrow? There wasn't enough light to see anybody very well. It looked like a man, dressed in Maasai red clothing, and a bunch of kids. Why would anybody be out so late with their . . . it was Ruth! Were those some of her brothers and sisters, and was that her father? Maybe she'd come to tell me that everything was fine. But why did they have a wheelbarrow with them? Then I saw why. There was a person in it! It was Ruth's mother.

I rushed to their side. Her mother was lying there in the wheelbarrow, limp, unmoving, her eyes closed. Was she . . . was she . . . ? Her eyes popped open and she screamed in pain, her face contorted and her whole body arching up! I felt my breath freeze in my throat.

Ruth's father and the *askari* started frantically yelling at each other. Ruth bent down and took her mother's hands, and the littlest of the children began sobbing.

I rushed to their side as the man began a frantic dialogue with the *askari*. I stood there, helpless, listening but not understanding. I knew it was desperate, it was bad, and that I needed to just keep my mouth shut. It had to do with the baby. Was she still in labour, was that what it was?

She closed her eyes again and her body went limp. Everybody else kept arguing and crying and—

"Everybody stop!" I screamed. I was shocked when everybody stopped talking and listened.

"I need to know what's happening. I need to know what's wrong."

Ruth's father started talking to me in rapid-fire Swahili.

"*Hakuna . . . kizungu!*" I yelled, telling him I needed English.

He stopped, turned to Ruth, and spoke to her. She nodded.

"My mother . . . the baby can't come out . . . she needs help."

"But there's nobody here but me! The others won't be back for hours!"

"Not wait for hours. She needs to get to the clinic."

"The clinic? Where's the clinic?"

"By the market in Emali."

I shook my head. "I don't know where that is."

"Twenty miles along the road."

"That's not too far. Maybe we can call for an ambu—" No phones. There were no phones. There probably wasn't an ambulance, either.

Ruth's mother shrieked in pain again and I felt it through my whole body.

"My mother will die without help . . . the baby will die."

"But, but, I don't know what to do," I pleaded.

"The car," Ruth said. "She needs to be driven."

I turned around. Of course! They could borrow the car! There was nobody to ask, but who could object? This was an emergency, life and death, and he was a chief! I ran over to the car, just hoping that the keys were—yes, they were in the ignition!

"Come, come, quickly, get her in the car!" I ran to the back and lifted up the hatch. There was a flat spot where she could lie down. I saw a blanket draped over the back seat so I grabbed it and placed it on the floor. At least she'd have something soft to lie on . . . like that would soften the blows of a thousand bumps between here and where they had to go.

Ruth's father started to move the wheelbarrow but the three *askari* blocked his way! They began arguing loudly, gesturing, screaming at each other.

"Ruth, what's happening?"

"They say they can't let the car go. They do not have permission!"

The argument got louder and Ruth's father stepped back, pushed aside his tunic, and pulled out his *konga!*

"Stop!" I screamed. I stepped between them and turned to face the *askari*.

"She is going into the car," I said. "I am in charge here, they left me in charge, and I am giving them permission to take the car."

They all looked confused, but nobody seemed convinced. Time for a good offence.

"Step aside immediately! I am ordering the two of you to leave! If you do not listen, you will be canned! Do you understand?"

They didn't look like they understood.

I turned to Ruth. "I need a word. 'Canned.'" No, she

wouldn't know what that meant. "'Terminated' . . . do you know 'terminated'?"

She shook her head.

"Their jobs will *die!*"

"Oh! *Itakufa,*" Ruth said.

"Good. Step aside right now, or I will *itakufa* all of you!" I shouted.

The eyes of all three widened in recognition. I'd obviously gotten their attention, but they still didn't move. I needed to say something more.

"What's the word for 'fired'?" I asked Ruth.

"*Moto.*"

"All three of you listen to me or I—me—will make sure you all *itakufa!* Get out of the way, now, or I will *moto* all of you! Do you understand me? *Itakufa*—I will *moto* all of you!"

They practically jumped aside. Ruth's father picked her mother up out of the wheelbarrow. She grimaced in pain and her whole body seemed to stiffen. He laid her down and put his face against her ear. He was whispering something. I couldn't hear, and I wouldn't have known what the words meant anyway, but I did know that he was offering her reassurance. He stood up and I closed the door.

"The keys are in the ignition," I said to Ruth. "You can leave your brothers and sisters here and I'll take care of them."

"No," Ruth said, shaking her head. "You must come along."

"There's not much I can do, and I really should be here to explain things to the staff when they get back."

"You don't understand. My father doesn't know how to drive. You must drive us."

"Me? I'm only fifteen . . . I don't have a driver's licence."

"But can you drive? Do you know how?"

"Yes of course, technically, and I have driven, but surely somebody else knows how to drive." I looked at the three *askari*. "Do any of you know how to drive?"

They all shook their heads. We had a car—a four-wheel-drive jeep—we had the keys, and the only person who knew how to drive was me. That was just plain crazy. But what were the choices?

"Get in!" I yelled. "Ruth, you get in the back seat, and your father should come up front so he can give me directions. The kids stay here. You three," I said, pointing at the *askari,* "are going to babysit them. Ruth, what word am I looking for?"

"*Angalia.*"

"Take care of the children. *Angalia!* Understand?"

They all nodded obediently. That was more like it.

"Now, let's get going."

I almost got in on the wrong side of the car before I caught myself and climbed in behind the wheel. Ruth's father got in beside me. He placed his spear on the floor of he car, angling it between the two seats. I turned the key and the engine came to life. So far so good.

I thought about my driving lessons. I was only two short of finishing the course. I'd just think of this as another lesson. The only differences were that I had a Maasai warrior beside me instead of an instructor, I was on the wrong side of the car getting ready to drive on the wrong side of the road, the road had more in common with a goat path than a paved road, I was in Africa, it was night, and I had a pregnant, possibly dying woman in the back. Almost exactly the same. I adjusted the rear-view mirror, snapped on my seatbelt, and put it into drive.

The car rocketed forward. I'd given it too much gas and so I hit the brake, made the curve around the driveway, and drove for the gate. Wasn't it wider than that? I aimed for the middle, well aware that touching either side would send electricity into the metal car. We slipped through the opening. I looked back through my rear-view mirror as the *askari* started to close the gate behind us.

The path out of the compound was rough, but I knew it was probably the best stretch of road we were going to be on for the whole trip. I skidded to a stop at the road.

"Which way?" I called out.

Ruth's father gestured to the left, back toward their village, the opposite direction from where everybody had gone tonight. Somehow, for a split second, I had thought that we might be able to run into them and Renée would be able to take care of everything. No such luck.

We hit the first big bump and only my seatbelt stopped me from flying into the air. Ruth's mother wasn't so lucky and she cried out in pain as she landed again. I'd have to be careful. I couldn't put her through extra pain. I also couldn't risk putting us off the road or she'd never get there—or maybe all of us would have to be taken to the clinic. The headlights stretched out ahead of us, illuminating the road. It was like a little oasis of light in a gigantic desert. All around there was nothing but dark.

Ruth's father turned around and said something to Ruth. She nodded.

"My father wants to know if you really would have done it, done what you said, to those *askari.*"

"It was more like a threat, but I would have tried."

"And how would you have done it?" she asked. "How would you have put them in a fire and killed them?"

"Killed them? Put them in a fire?"

"Yes, how would you have put them into a fire?"

"A fire . . . no . . . you don't understand . . . there wasn't anything about a fire. I was going to fire them from their jobs. I wasn't going to kill them, I was going to get them fired, make them lose their jobs!"

"But that is not what you said to them. You told them you would make them die by putting them in a fire."

"I didn't know . . . I was just using the words you told me."

"Yes. You told them you would make them die if they did not get out of the way."

"But that wasn't what I was trying to say . . . oh, who cares, it worked!"

She smiled. "I will not tell my father that you used the words wrong. He respected you very much that you would kill them. Besides, what you did, you saved their lives."

"How did I do that?"

"If you had not made them move, my father *was* going to kill them."

I looked back over the seat at her for just a split second and then back to the road and I jumped on the brakes! There was a gigantic gully in front of us. I brought us to a stop before we could bottom out. This was really something. Not only was I driving without a licence, but technically I'd stolen the car, or at least taken it without permission, and now I'd found out that I'd threatened to kill three people who were trying to stop me. I didn't even want to think what was going to happen to me.

I inched the car down the gully and it bounced and Ruth's mother screamed in pain. I didn't have time to think about what was going to happen to me.

—

With each bump I braced myself. Not just for the flight but for the cry of pain it would bring. After a while I guess I was becoming desensitized because her cries didn't cut as deeply into me. Then I realized that wasn't it. Her cries weren't as sharp, weren't as strong. It could have been that she was becoming more used to the ride, or maybe she wasn't in as much pain, but I didn't think so. I thought she was getting weaker. My initial fear that she might give birth in the car was replaced by something even more traumatic. She might die in the car—right there before my eyes—and it would be my fault because I didn't get her to the clinic soon enough.

"Can you go faster?" Ruth asked.

"I'm moving as quickly as I can. I can't see the road in the dark. I'm doing the best I can. How is your mother doing?"

Ruth didn't answer.

"Ruth, how is she doing?"

"I think you need to drive faster."

"If I do, the ride will get rougher. It will be more difficult for her."

"Please," she said, "she needs to get help."

I looked in the rear-view mirror and I could see Ruth. She looked scared. I wanted to say something to her, tell her that everything was fine, that it would all work out, that her mother would be okay. I couldn't say any of that. I just didn't know, and I wasn't going to lie to her.

The engine growled as we picked up speed. Another bump was coming up, I was certain of that, but what choice was there? Driving slowly was just going to lead to a slow death. The car rocked back and forth as I moved across the road, trying to find the best, smoothest course. We hit a bump and all of us caught air. She cried out in pain. I was almost grateful.

"How much longer?" I asked.

"We're more than halfway," Ruth said, "a lot more."

"This is ridiculous! Nobody should be this far away from help. You need a clinic right near the village."

"No money for clinic," Ruth said.

"This shouldn't be about money! People shouldn't die because of a few crummy dollars!" I shouldn't have said that . . . about dying . . . but it was what we were all thinking, anyway.

I slammed on the brakes, skidding the car sideways. There was a gigantic gorge in the road where a stream had washed away the whole side. I inched us forward, the bottom of the car scraping as we hit, and started slowly up the other side.

I wanted to pray, but I couldn't close my eyes. God would understand. *Please, God, just let us get there safely. Let her be okay. Let the baby be okay. Amen. Please. Please. Please.*

"There it is!" Ruth screamed. "We're here!"

The headlights bounced against the front of a building, small and brown and one storey tall, not big, and all dark. If this was *it,* what was it? I pulled the car up to the front door and leaned on the horn, hard and long. The sound broke through the darkness and bounced back off the front of the building.

Ruth's father jumped from the car almost before it had

stopped moving. He ran to the front door and began
pounding on it, screaming at the top of his lungs. Almost
immediately a light came on in one of the windows, and
then a second, and a third! Whoever was there was now
awake!

"Let's help get your mother out of the car."

We climbed out and circled to the back. I was almost
afraid of what we'd find. I opened up the hatch. Her eyes
were open and she smiled—a sad, brave smile. I offered her
my hand and she took it. Gently, slowly, she rocked to a sitting position, and we helped her get to her feet. The whole
back of the car was covered in blood! Her red dress was
stained with blood!

She was all hunched over, almost like she was
cradling the baby inside of her. She shuffled forward, little steps, with one of us on each side supporting her.
Ruth's father was standing at the door, which was open.
Light streamed out. He was talking to a woman. I hoped
she was a nurse, or better yet, a doctor. They were talking.
No, they were arguing.

"What's going on?" I asked Ruth.

"She says my mother is not a patient at the clinic so
she cannot help her. She is saying go to the clinic down
the road."

"There's another clinic? Where is it?"

"Along the road. Maybe twenty more miles."

"That's impossible," I said. "This isn't going to happen.
Let's help your mother to sit." We eased her to the ground,
right at the doorway.

"You!" I demanded. "Do you speak English?"

She nodded her head. "I speak English. This man does
not understand that his wife cannot—"

"Are you a nurse?"

"Yes, I am a nurse."

"Good. Now we're going to take this woman inside and you're going to help her."

"You do not understand. This woman is not—"

"No, *you* do not understand. This woman is in need of medical assistance and you are going to help her. And if you don't, do you understand what a lawsuit is?"

I got the feeling that she didn't.

"If you don't help this woman right now and something happens to her, I will make sure that you will lose your job, that you will lose your licence to be a nurse, and I'm going to work to make sure you are put in jail! Do *you* understand *that?*" I yelled.

Her mouth was moving but no words were coming out. "I . . . I do not have permission to let her—"

"Permission? You're a nurse! Did you train to help people or to send them away to die? Could you live with yourself if that happened? Look at the woman. She needs your help."

The woman put her hand up to her face and rubbed it against her jaw. She looked at Ruth's mother. She bent down beside her and placed her hand against the side of her neck, feeling for a pulse. She looked as though she really wanted to help.

"Where do you want us to bring her?" I asked.

"Inside. Follow."

Ruth and I pulled her mother to her feet and started to lead her in.

"I thought you were going to threaten to kill her, too," Ruth said quietly.

"That was next."

We eased her through the door and followed the light down a corridor. Ruth's father, spear in hand, followed.

There was no danger of me actually killing anybody, but I wouldn't have made any assumptions about him.

"Here, place her here," the woman said. She was standing beside a rusty metal table with a dingy brown pad on the top.

We eased her up on the top and she laid back, her belly bulging out in front of her. There was a thin trail of blood making its way down her legs. *Maybe,* I thought, *we should leave.* As I took a step, Ruth grabbed me by the arm and I knew I needed to be there.

The nurse did an examination, moving her hands around, asking questions. She then turned to us. "There is nothing I can do."

"What do you mean there's nothing you can do? You promised you'd help."

"I cannot help. The baby is turned and I cannot make it come out. We need the doctor."

"Where is he?" I demanded.

"He is sleeping. In a house in back."

"Then we have to wake him up. Which house?"

"More," she said, "he needs to operate . . . open her . . . he needs medicine . . . antiseptic . . . anaesthetic, much, *much* money."

"Money?" I said, and I started to laugh. They all looked at me like I was crazy. "You need money?" I pulled open my purse and pulled out a wad of bills. I threw the bills onto the counter and they scattered. "Is this enough?"

She looked at the money, then at the patient, and then at me. "I will get the doctor."

CHAPTER TWENTY

I heard the truck before I could see it. Then I saw the headlights bumping up the road. I couldn't actually see that it
was them, but who else could it be? Maybe I should have
gotten up and welcomed them, but I was too exhausted,
too spent to even move. I stayed seated on the step of the
clinic's porch.

The gears ground loudly as the truck slowed down and
it pulled into the spot beside the jeep, the headlights shin-
ing right into my face. I used my arm to shield my eyes.
The lights clicked off, the engine died, and the two doors
popped open. Renée and Nebala jumped out and ran
toward me.

"Are you all right?" Renée yelled.

"I'm fine. Everybody is all right. Mother and new
baby daughter. They're inside." I had an urge to say something about her makeup—she looked really good—but I
thought this probably wasn't the time or place.

Renée let out a gigantic sigh. "Thank goodness."

"The baby was breech," I said, trying to explain. "They couldn't turn it and it couldn't come out. They were both going to die. The doctor had to operate."

"You should have waited for us to return," she said.

"The doctor said they would have been dead if he hadn't operated when he did. Ruth's mother would have bled to death. Ruth is donating blood for her right now," I said, gesturing to the door. "How much trouble am I in?"

"You shouldn't have threatened to kill the *askari*."

"I didn't mean that. I was trying to tell them I was going to get them fired, not kill them by putting them in a fire!" I protested.

Nebala chuckled.

"I thought there might have been something lost in the translation," Renée said.

"I just didn't have any choice. I needed to take the car."

"*Steal* the car."

"*Borrow* the car. It's right there. It's okay . . . maybe the suspension isn't so good . . . I'll pay to get it fixed."

"It wasn't good to start, and there's no point in fixing it. The next trip would just knock it out of whack again. But Alexandria, you really went out on a limb here. You could have killed yourself, or all of them."

"It wasn't like I was out joyriding. What choice did I have?"

"Not much, I guess."

"So, how much trouble am I in? What are you going to put in the report to the judge?"

"I've already written most of it," Renée said. "I wrote about how hard you worked, how you connected to the local people, how much growth I've seen, and how proud I am of who you are in the process of becoming."

"And now?"

"I hate rewriting things. Besides, now I have proof that what I was saying is true. I'm very proud of you . . . *really.*"

"Which part are you most proud of, stealing the car, driving without a licence, or threatening to kill those three men?"

"All three. Equally."

"I hope the judge feels the same way."

"Some things even a judge doesn't need to know."

The nurse appeared at the door. "They want to see you," she said to me.

I stood up and my legs got all wobbly and I felt as though I might topple over. Renée reached out and steadied me.

"How about if I come along?" she suggested.

"I think that might be good."

She held me by the arm and we walked into the clinic, along the corridor to the little back section. There were two beds—the clinic's capacity—and Ruth and her mother were there. Ruth was lying in one bed giving blood, and her mother was in the other, nursing the newborn. I had never seen a baby so small. It was *so tiny.*

Her mother motioned for me to come closer. I walked to her bedside. She took the baby and offered it to me to hold. I hesitated.

"Go on," Renée said. "Don't worry. You won't drop her."

Carefully, slowly, I took the little girl, all wrapped in a rough blue blanket, and pulled her toward me. She was so little it was like holding air. She was so small. So precious. So alive.

Ruth's mother spoke. I couldn't tell what she was saying.

"She said that the baby is yours," Renée explained.

"Mine? But I can't bring a baby back with me!"

"Not to bring back," Renée said. "She'll stay here, but as far as the family is concerned, she's yours."

"Okay . . . *asante sana.*"

"My mother also asks how you spell your name," Ruth said.

"Do they need it for the hospital forms?"

Ruth shook her head. "They need your name for the birth certificate. My baby sister, her name is Alexandria."

I was stunned. I looked down at the little baby in my arms.

"What do you think?" Renée asked.

"I like it. Alexandria . . . Alexandria of Africa."

CHAPTER TWENTY-ONE

I pulled my suitcase off the conveyor belt. The rest of my luggage and the remainder of my clothing had stayed behind. I could always buy more here, if I wanted to. There were at least two or three stores that must have been close to going out of business without me around for the last few weeks. I'd fix that as soon as possible. I'd call my friends and we could go out shopping—of course, I'd warn them that they were going to have to hear some of my stories first.

Everybody around me seemed to be moving so quickly. I wasn't in that big a rush. Don't get me wrong, I was really looking forward to seeing my parents—I just wasn't in a big hurry. I stopped at the doors leading out to Arrivals, where everybody waited. Some other passengers just breezed through the doors and I could see throngs of people waiting just outside, just past the barrier. It was time.

I pulled my bag along. There seemed to be thousands of people standing around, staring, craning their necks, holding signs, hoping and waiting. Some had already connected and were hugging or shaking hands. Where were my parents? I'd expected my mother would be here, at least . . . and hopefully my father was able to get off work to meet me.

"Alexandria!"

I turned, searching for the voice, searching for my mother. She—and my father—were rushing toward me, waving and yelling! I ran toward them and we met in a big group hug. I could feel my mother sobbing and knew I wasn't far from tears myself.

"It's so wonderful to see you!" my mother cried. She then tilted her head to one side and looked at me strangely. "Poor dear, you look so tired."

"I'm not. I slept on the plane."

"No, your mother's right, your eyes look tired . . ."

"I'm just not wearing much makeup, that's all."

"Then you *must* be exhausted," my mother said.

I tried not to laugh. "I feel fine, honestly."

"And your hair, what happened to your hair?"

"Nothing happened to my hair. I just tied it back like this for the flight."

"Well, it looks quite . . . *different* that way. And that bandana . . . it looks so . . . so *quaint*."

"I'm glad you like it. I got one for you, too."

Her eyes widened in shock.

"Just kidding," I said, and she looked relieved.

"Don't worry, we'll just set up an appointment for you with Mr. Henri. I'll tell him it's an emergency."

And I realized that my mother had no idea what a *real* emergency was.

"That's okay, I really don't . . . well . . . maybe that would be good."

"That's my baby!" she said.

I was and I wasn't, but there was no point in trying to explain it. There was so much I had to explain, so much I wanted to tell, so much I was still trying to understand myself.

"Where's the rest of your luggage?" my father asked. "Don't tell me the airline lost it."

I shook my head. "I left the other bags behind, along with most of my clothes."

"Alexandria, those were all new clothes. You can't expect us to just run out and buy you—"

"I don't need anything new," I said, cutting my father off. "I've already got more clothes than I need."

My father and mother exchanged a stunned look. I almost laughed, just looking at them. I didn't know how I could explain it to them, but I'd try. In time.

"I have something you do need," my father said. "Your mother wanted me to wait until your birthday, but I thought, what the heck, it's only a week away."

He held out his hand, dangling a key and a keychain with a Mercedes emblem in front of my eyes. He dropped it in my hand.

"It's a CLK 350 . . . Cabriolet . . . a convertible . . . white. Very stylish, like the girl who'll be driving it!"

I didn't know what to say. It was exactly the car I'd dreamed about and schemed for. And now I was holding the key in my hand.

"We can pick it up from the dealership on the morning of your birthday!" he exclaimed.

"So . . . you haven't actually taken the car yet, right?"

"We've signed the papers and everything is set, but the sale isn't final until delivery. Why?"

"I was just wondering . . . and I know this is going to sound ungrateful . . . but do I have to have *that* car?"

"Alexandria, I know it's not the *very* top of the line, but you can't expect me to spend any more money than—"

"No," I said, cutting him off. "I was wondering if you could spend *less.*"

"Less?" both my parents said in perfect unison, with identical looks of utter confusion. They couldn't have looked more lost if I'd spoken to them in Swahili. Less . . . *kasa . . . kasoro.* Actually, they didn't look confused, they looked worried, almost scared.

"I really do want a car," I said, and they both relaxed a bit. "I just don't need a Mercedes. I was thinking a Mustang."

"I thought that was the one car you *didn't* want," my father said.

"Carmella likes hers. It would be a lot less money, right?"

"About a third of the cost of the Mercedes," my father said, and chuckled.

"Then there would be some left over if I wanted some money."

My father smiled. This was something he understood, something that was familiar.

"How much did you have in mind?"

"Well, I'm not exactly sure, but I was thinking around twenty thousand dollars."

"Twenty thousand dollars! That's a lot of money for me to just give you!"

"Your father's right, Alexandria."

"No, you don't understand. I don't want you to give me a cent."

"Who do you want me to give the money to?" he questioned.

"It isn't really a *who* as much as a *what,* a place." I paused. "This is hard to explain, but I really need you to understand . . . both of you."

"We're listening," my father said, and I could tell that they really *were* listening.

"You see, there's this community, and there are no hospitals, and they need our help . . . your help . . . and I was just wondering . . ."

AFTERWORD

Alexandria of Africa was mostly written while I was in Kenya with my son, Nick. We were there, in part, with an amazing organization called Free The Children. My son had raised $20,000 for a school to be built in memory of his Uncle Peter, who had died of cancer. We were part of the opening ceremony at that school as well as helping to actually build another school.

A great deal of the things we experienced, participated in, and witnessed form "the bones" of this book. Nebala is real. Renée is real—although she has much better fashion sense in real life—and the Renée character in my book is a combination of her and another amazing individual, Robin, who also works for Free The Children. They kindly allowed me dramatic licence to re-create their personalities in these pages.

Being in Africa was truly one of the most amazing experiences of my life. It was wonderful to be there with an organization that is dedicated to changing the lives of young people around the world. For more information about how you become involved with Free The Children go to www.freethechildren.com.

ERIC WALTERS, a former elementary school teacher, began writing as a way to encourage his students to become more enthusiastic about literature. His young adult novels have won numerous awards, including the Silver Birch, Blue Heron, Red Maple, Snow Willow, and Ruth Schwartz. He lives in Mississauga, Ontario. His website is www.ericwalters.net.